BULLFIDDLER

BULLFIDDLER

The True Adventures of a Texas Bass Player

David Leibson

Copyright © 2008 by David Leibson.

ISBN: Softcover   978-1-4363-7018-9

All rights reserved. No part of this book may be reproduced or transmitted in any form or by any means, electronic or mechanical, including photocopying, recording, or by any information storage and retrieval system, without permission in writing from the copyright owner.

This is an autobiographical aspect of 20th century Texas music history. All characters, places and incidents mentioned existed in the Latin and Texas music world. Only the characteristics of the 'Bullfiddler' came from the author's imagination.

This is also a story of recovery.

This book was printed in the United States of America.

To order additional copies of this book, contact:
Xlibris Corporation
1-888-795-4274
www.Xlibris.com
Orders@Xlibris.com
53433

Contents

ACKNOWLEDGEMENTS 9
INTRODUCTION 11

1. FIRST GIG 15
2. FIRST GUITAR 18
3. THE DOWNBEATS 20
4. EL PASO MUSIC 24
5. JUAREZ MUSIC 27
6. THE BUST 31
7. A SMUGGLING MOMMA 33
8. ESCAPING EL PASO 39
9. AUSTIN TEXAS 44
10. A TEXAS MUSIC SCHOOL 49
11. OPEN MICS 51
12. FIRED! 53
13. CURLEY 56
14. MUSIC THERAPY 59
15. RECORDING IN AUSTIN 62
16. BOOKING GIGS 68
17. BLAZE FOLEY 76
18. CHAMP'S PIANO 80
19. WILLIE'S PICNIC 84
20. THE GREAT JESSIE TAYLOR 86
21. BILINGUAL TEXAS MUSIC 91
22. THE BLACK CAT 94
23. INTERVIEWING WILLIE 96
24. SURVIVORS 99
25. KERRVILLE KERVERT 101
26. THE MARRYING KIND 104
27. DIAMOND SIMON 106
28. REHAB AND RECOVERY 110
29. GETTING RELIGION 117
30. TEXAS WICCANS AND QUAKERS 121

EPILOG 123

DEDICATION

This book is dedicated to Sigmund, Brandie and Isiah, true friends. It is also dedicated to Charles Polacheck, one of the few remaining survivors of the original Weavers.

Acknowledgements

I want to take this opportunity to thank Michael Libby, Christy Parks and Erika Garcia with Xlibris for their help in getting this project done. I also want to thank the musicians I am currently playing with for their patience and understanding. Maryjane Ford is a guitar playing, banjo strumming band leader with humility and a good sense of direction, Jim Barry on piano loves the oldies (50 and 60's) as much as I do and is very quiet when not playing piano, Mark Skrabacz is an excellent harmonica player and spiritual guide who finds wonderful out of town gigs and Ed Slagel is the quietest fiddler to have ever played music. Thanks to Tom Martin for all his formatting abilities. Cudos to Regan Marie Brown, whose book 'The Woman's Way' is applicable to men as well as women, and whose photo graces the cover of this book.

David Leibson

Introduction

One cannot possibly convey the excitement of playing music before thousands at Auditorium Shores or Eeyore's Birthday party in Austin, Texas. Nor can one truly express the thrill of holding an original recording in your hands knowing it will be marketed to complete strangers for years to come. It is impossible to describe adequately the trials of making bilingual recordings in the heart of Texas or the satisfaction of working with fine, talented musicians both on stage and in the recording studio. Yet, these events are daily occurrences for hundreds of working musicians at all levels, from symphony bassoonists to swing fiddles, Cajun accordions to church fiddlers, not to mention great guitarists. I have tried to capture some of the excitement I have found playing and recording music in Austin and the surrounding small towns.

Live music venues are all over Austin and in the many small hamlets that surround Austin such as The Oaks in Elgin, Giddy Ups in Manchaca, Poodies in Spicewood, The Little Wheel near Dripping Springs and of course the Kerrville Folk Festival. There are countless clubs, honky tonks and restaurants like The Poodle Dog, Nuevo Leon, Old Ross' Cafe and Sam's that have live music and do not publicize in the newspapers.

There are more than 200 live music venues in Austin according to the Austin American Statesman, and those are the ones that advertise. Travis County has countless other clubs, churches, recovery clubs and benefits that offer live music for free or for a small contribution to the tip jar. Many venues, like Artz Ribhouse, Central Market, Flipnotics, Ginny's Little Longhorn Saloon, Blues on the Green and Eeyore's don't charge a dime for admission. According to the Austin telephone book yellow pages there are 44 recording studios and CD manufacturers, quadruple the number in Nashville, (there are hundreds more listings in The Austin Music Directory). Sitting in each recording studio are vaults full of thousands of recordings that began there but for reasons such as artist preparedness or money never saw completion and there are countless home studios using computers that are making recordings comparable in quality to anything you might find commercially. Music magazines for different music styles spring up and fold in Austin annually, as do bands of various styles. Some acts make it, some don't. There is a large music support system in Austin that deals with every aspect of music.

Austin has the Austin Music Foundation, a Music Industry Boot Camp, The Simms Program (a musician health program), Friends of Traditional Music, the Austin Music Office, the Health Alliance for Austin Musicians, Austin School of Music, the Austin Federation of Musicians, the state sponsored Texas Music Coalition, South Austin Music (on line), the Austin Music Connection and All Texas Music.com (MP3 distribution). All of these agencies are staffed with workers, as are the numerous rehearsal and recording halls and studios, each offering exciting jobs in the music field that do not involve playing music. All of the above are open to the public and offer services from recording to promotion, health care, gigs and supplies.

The music industry worldwide is fraught with danger when one mixes drugs with the industry. In the 1960's booze, pot and LSD were staples of the industry. These days there is Meth, Rohipnol and Ecstasy that are readily available and often addictive. There are almost fifty AA groups in Travis County along with Texas and Austin-Travis County Mental Health and Mental Retardation facilities that deal with these problems, not to mention the psychiatric hospitals. Recovery is not easy but unlike many other towns there are ample facilities available for those that need to clean up. There are hundreds of drug and alcohol-free musicians in Austin, but the temptations will always be there. Austin has many recovering working musicians, there is a wealth of good role models and an abundance of positive promises of the numerous good experiences available to the recovering music industry employee. I by no means want to imply that the Austin music scene is rife with substance abuse problems, but they are there and for a young novice from say, Wink or Dime Box Texas, the temptations can be hard to ignore, and the dangers are very real.

It would take pages to describe the availability of live national touring acts that come to perform and record in Austin. More national and international acts constantly fill UT performance halls and large venues like the Long Center or the Erwin Center in and around Austin. Musical plays can be found daily at theaters around town, and it is not uncommon to run into many of these performers on their off hours at the numerous restaurants in Austin. The Austin Chronicle and The Austin American Statesman XL editions both come out each Thursday with long lists of both local and national acts appearing in Austin seven days a week, every day of the year. There is no shortage of any type of music for the music lover.

Austin has one of the best economies in America. Recessions and Depressions do not hit Austin like they do in other American towns but the current economy is beginning to have a small but real impact on the Austin music scene. There are, according to the current Austin telephone book more than twenty music stores in Travis county, each with their own faithful employees and clientele and some are bound to suffer during this historic economic slowdown. El Paso songwriter Tom Russell said it best in his song 'It Goes Away' :

> "One day, it might take years
> or a hundred thousand tears
> but one day the sky's will clear and
> it will go away."

Austin music is more alive than it was when I arrived here in 1982. The growth has been phenomenal and it is hard to imagine the music industry in Austin slowing down. Living in Austin for the past 26 years has been one long memorable adventure and the best is yet to come.

Chapter 1

FIRST GIG

The Bullfiddler had his first musical gig singing three songs in Hebrew, acapella on his Bar Mitzvah at Temple Mount Saini in El Paso, Texas in 1959. Bullfiddler just turned 13, Elvis was hitting big in El Paso and sock hops at Coldwell Elementary School near the geographic center of El Paso featured not only Elvis music, but that of Jerry Lee Lewis, the Everly Brothers, Gene Vincent, Hank Williams and other rockers of the period. The Bullfiddler was listening to 'Be Bob A Lula' while studying for his Bar Mitzvah.

At the sock hops public school students were required by school officials to take off their shoes so they wouldn't scuff up the gymnasium floor. Dancing couples always had bodily contact with our dance partner. Couples held hands and jitterbugged on the fast dances like 'Hound Dog' or 'Be Bop a Lula' and couples clung together during the slow songs like 'Donna' or 'Dream'. There was a street dress code for the 1950's that occasionally conflicted with the dress code of the school. The boys had greased back hair usually slicked with Vitalis or crew cuts and short hair with the hair on the front brushed to stand straight up and wore white tee shirts with the sleeves rolled up. The girls wore dresses that passed their knees, white bobby sox and a ponytail, not unlike the girls in televisions 'Happy Days'. Cigarette smoking and 'Spin the Bottle' were standard behaviors by 1958.

By 1959 everyone in 5th grade at Coldwell Elementary knew 'Jack the Juvie' who moved into a house at the dead end of El Paso's Cambridge Avenue. Jack Wrunkle had served time in Gatesville boys prison while in his elementary school years. Bullfiddler met Jack when the Bullfiddler was in fifth grade at school. Jack taught many in his age group how to smoke cigarettes and play "spin the bottle' with the neighborhood girls. Jack was a real 'Fonzie' at that time with his jet black slicked back hair with a Little Richard type pompadour hanging over his forehead. He always wore blue jeans and a black leather jacket. Only, unlike the Fonz on TV, Jack could be mean; he was eventually shot and killed during a robbery of a pawnshop on Dyer Street in northeast El Paso.

The Bullfiddler learned how to smoke cigarettes and drink alcoholic beverages while listening to 45 RPM records on a cheap plastic phonograph in his neighbor Stanley's garage. The phonograph had a regular spindle so the kids had to swap out the plastic fillers that were necessary in order to hear the 45's correctly. The 45's were popular at the time and could withstand the constant dust storms that often raged out of the desert that swirled around the foothills of the Franklin and Juarez Mountains. All this was before cassettes or CD's and the more the records were played the scratchier they sounded. The Bullfiddler was not yet focusing in on the music and bass lines but he did listen Buddy Holly, The Ventures, Roy Orbison and others on the new popular battery operated portable transistor radios. During the World Series a lot of guys in Bullfiddlers fifth grade class were 'tuned in' to the games with the ear piece coming out of their shirt collar and into their ear.

During the 1950's El Paso had one rock and roll station KELP. Steve Crosno was known city-wide as a hard core rocking DJ in the southwest next to Wolfman Jack who was broadcasting loud, hot and heavy out of Mexico. Crosno died in Las Cruces New Mexico in 2007. He was buried in Las Cruces, but in 1957 he and Wolfman Jack played this new rebellious rock and roll during school hours and late into the El Paso nights. On the evening of October 29th, 1959 the Bullfiddler sang the bread and wine prayers acapella in Hebrew and the Kaddish before over 350 dusty El Pasoans.

Jewish boys and girls had to sing these prayers and other chants but the Bullfiddler doesn't remember having much stage fright that Friday night. The lack of stage fear might be due to the fact that all the material was so well rehearsed and the Bullfiddler was accompanied on stage by his father and the Rabbi on that chilly windy October Friday night in El Paso's Reform congregation sanctuary. Bullfiddler could smell the aroma of the Mogan David wine sitting in the goblet on the pulpit and he remembered the bitter sweet taste of a wine he had never drank before that Friday night. An incident occurred during that second gig on Saturday afternoon when one of Bullfiddler's schoolmates was kicked out of the religious service by the Rabbi. The student took a good tongue lashing from the Rabbi in his study after the service for the students lack of respect for the service. People were getting thrown out of Bullfiddler's first gig. The Bullfiddler was paid more in gifts and Bar Mitzvah money for that weekend gig than he ever made playing music in El Paso or Austin.

The biggest frustration of the Bar Mitzvah affair was that Bullfiddler was not allowed to write his own speech. The boy's father, a career journalist/speech writer wrote Bullfiddler's speech for him and would not let Bullfiddler say anything on his own, not that Bullfiddler had anything to say that year. He was yet to read his first newspaper. The Bullfiddler was a 78 pound thirteen year old who knew little of world or local events. Even the way he learned to read Hebrew was different in other Jewish congregations. Children in the Conservative or Orthodox Jewish congregations knew how to read Hebrew by age thirteen but in the Reform branch the religious students studied their Torah and Hebrew prayers in English and phonetics. Reform students memorized the prayers and songs in both Hebrew and English.

Chapter 2

FIRST GUITAR

Bullfiddler's first guitar was a Stella F-hole steel string bought from El Pasoan Ronnie Saltzmn in 1962. The guitar had a thick wide neck and had a hairline crack running up the top side of the guitar soundbox. The strings had rust on them and felt rough to the touch. The Bullfiddler was fifteen, the guitar cost twenty dollars and came with a hand drawn diagram of the chords G,C and D along with the handwritten lyrics for 'Puff The Magic Dragon' and 'Michael'. Ronnie showed the boy how to tune the guitar and how to play those chords and the two songs. Bullfiddler then went home, typed out the song lyrics and hand wrote the chords on top of the word they changed, setting a musical precedent to last the rest of Bullfiddlers life.

Bullfiddler lived in a bedroom he shared with his younger brother and played through 'Puff' and 'Michael' for days until he could play it from beginning to end. The fingertips on his left chord making hand blistered and yet at this time the boy had no real desire to be play in public. Ronnie helped the boy learn other chords and other songs such as 'If I Had a Hammer' and 'This Train','Bound for Glory' and 'This Land is Your Land'. Bullfiddler obsessively played these songs over and over again in the bedroom and never once did his mother object. She was an old folkie with Josh White, Lenny Bruce and Woodie Guthrie albums along with a large collection of classical music of Russian classical composers. Bullfiddler's mother never played her records and she only interrupted the boy's self-imposed practice to announce it was time for the dinner. He could smell the aromas of the cooking coming from the kitchen. His mother was grateful her son was not running loose in downtown El Paso. Little did she know that her son would eventually play guitar three to four nights a week for three years in downtown El Paso.

At age fifteen young Bullfiddler did not feel like part of his high school crowd. He was underweight, wore glasses, did not have a car and because of an eye injury/operation in third grade was not sports minded. When a ball came toward him he could not accurately judge where the ball was and therefore could not catch a fly ball. He risked getting hit in the head with the ball, something Bullfiddler quickly developed an aversion to. The pain caused by the sun on the scar tissue on his right eyeball made it impossible to play in the sun, so with a doctors note Bullfiddler was excused by the school coaches from physical education games and exercises, spending his elementary school years sitting in the shade near the rank smelling garbage cans at the back door of Coldwell Grade School kitchen. That shady spot was where the coaches also sent kids for punishment so the Bullfiddler often had company and one of the 'bad boys' taught him how to catch live flys that hovered around the garbage cans. To accomplish this he cupped his hand about an inch above the sitting fly, quickly moved the scooped hand about two inches above the fly causing the startled fly to rise up into a quickly closed hand. This some musicians would say, calls for timing. Bullfiddler became a fair fly catcher by the end of fifth grade. He was a natural. When the sun went down, the boy's pain went away and he became alive, nocturnal and pain free. During this trying elementary school period he began sneaking out of the house after dinner or bed time to play in a pain-free world.

Without suitable athletic ability in high school, hanging in Bullfiddlers shared bedroom learning to play Peter Paul and Mary and Kingston Trio songs was more desirable than playing in the 100 degree plus dry dusty outdoor El Paso weather and much to her relief his mother knew where Bullfiddler was which may account for her absolute early rehearsal support.

During the summer of 1963 there was a coffee house in the basement of a church at the foot of Mt. Franklin where the Bullfiddler saw his first live guitar players while candles and incense filled the basement air with nice aromas. The El Paso Folk and Beat singers sang covers of The Kingston Trio, Woodie Guthrie, Pete Seeger and other folkies while local El Paso teenage bands like 'The Wild Ones' were playing live loud fast rock and roll for school dances after football games, often in the basement of the local YMCA on El Paso's Montana street. The boy had no desire to join a band, but he did participate in school choirs and he was beginning to be exposed to various forms of live music.

Bullfiddler's first love affair began and ended in the El Paso High School choir room.

Chapter 3

THE DOWNBEATS

Bullfiddler just turned sixteen when he met a short stocky pimple-scarred Italian-American drummer, Richard Lasini. The night before they met Bullfiddler and some friends went to the Bobby Fuller Teen Center on Montana street where the Bobby Fuller Four was the house band. Bullfighter was amazed at how well Bobby Fuller covered early Beatles tunes like 'I Wanna Hold Your Hand' or 'She Loves You' as well as his own originals, 'Loves Made a Fool of You' and 'I Fought the Law'. Richard and the Bullfiddler later covered 'I Fought the Law' in the key of C. It was at the Bobby Fuller Teen Center where the young Bullfiddler first saw black and white interracial couples dancing or smooching at their booths. Hispanic-Anglo couples in El Paso were a given.

The two very unlikely characters, Richard and the Bullfiddler met on a hot summer afternoon school carnival at Cathedral High School. They talked while standing on a railing separating sweaty smelly ponies kids rode around an enclosed circle. Their conversation turned to music. Bullfiddler learned that Richard had a new set of Ludwig drums in the basement of his parents house and like Bullfiddler, Richard had never played in a band. By this time both were thinking about music especially after Bullfiddler spent an evening at a Bobby Fuller Four gig.

Bobby Fuller was just becoming known nationally in July of 1966. He was in Los Angeles at the crossroads of his life but his band was disintegrating. The day before his death Bobby had a fistfight with his brother Randy over a gig scheduled the following week in San Francisco, and Bobby was seriously considering firing his band and refilling all the positions. Bobby's body was discovered by his mother Lorraine and El Paso friend and drummer Ty Grimes. Fuller's death was ruled accidental even though when his body was found it was bruised and covered with gasoline, something people who knew the vane Fuller said he would never do. Rumors flew that Fuller who was performing in such LA clubs as P.J.'s, It's Boss and La Cave Pigalle (the Pig) was killed by goons hired by a rival club owner. His hit "I Fought The Law' was later covered by the Clash and Tom Petty and the Heartbreakers but the Fuller hit was originally written by Buddy Holly's Cricket and friend Sonny Curtis.

Fuller's manager at the time of his death was Bob Keane who also discovered and signed Richie Valens and Sam Cooke; Fuller was in experienced managerial hands even though Keane and Fuller fought often about Fullers musical style. When Bullfiddler saw Bobby Fuller at Fuller's El Paso teen club the Rendezvous, Fuller was only 20.

Austin's Michael Corcoran, a music critic said of Bobby Fuller: "Many extraordinary people are felled before they have a chance to reach their potential. Many leave the world without artistic proof that they ever existed. But Bobby Fuller left his mark with a sound and a song that will eternally epitomize defiant Texas guitar players. His voice was the sharp wail of a man who know what he wanted but couldn't break through the walls". What Bullfiddler remembered most was the excellent vocal harmonies of the Bobby fuller Four. The next day Bullfiddler met Lasini.

Richard was in his early twenties while the Bullfiddler was 16. Richard knew nothing about drums and at the time Bullfiddler had a clean F-hole Framus guitar with a plastic pick guard with low action under steel strings. Richard invited Bullfiddler to bring his guitar over to his basement for a 'jam session'. When the boy showed up the next day Richard had his drums set up in the basement that felt damp compared to the dry El Paso outdoors. The cramped basement was where Richard, the Bullfiddler and later Bobby Parker would rehearse and develop a stage show, but at their first session the two could not hear the guitar because the drums were so loud. Richard took a tape recorder's microphone wedged it in the F-Hole of the guitar and somehow via the tape recorder, the guitar was electrified. One of their first problems was that Richard detested folk songs and had a strong Italian desire to rock; the Bullfiddler did not know any rockers.

The two future rockers discussed a few songs and the young budding guitarist told Richard of some records he had at home, suggesting they try to work up some tunes. Bullfiddler went home, listened to the Rolling Stone's song 'Satisfaction' over and over, wrote down the lyrics, wrote the chords where the changes occurred and brought the song back to Richard. Those two must have played though that song hundreds of times with the tape recorder microphone knocking inside Bullfiddlers guitar. The pattern was set for the rest of their musical relationship. The two would find a song and the Bullfiddler would type up the lyrics and the music in the key it was played on the recording, transposing when necessary to fit Richards vocal range. A month after Bullfiddler and Richard met, Bobby Parker, an El Paso High School classmate of Bullfiddlers joined the group and in a week of daily rehearsals they had five songs they could roughly play through from beginning to end. Richard was becoming a stickler for clean song endings.

Bobby Parker was a skinny kid and a Beatles and Bob Dylan fan and he soon began bringing in songs to the group. Richard rejected out of hand any Dylan tunes because 'they did not rock'. Richard was becoming a macho task master once the trio decided to form a band and on occasion Richard threatened to kick some ass if they didn't rehearse daily as soon as school let out. Richard had completed three years in the Navy and was a cook at a junior high school three blocks from El Paso High School. He would meet Bobby and Bullfiddler at the bottom of the ramp that led up hill to the gray, three story prison looking El Paso High School at 3:30 when school let out. Richard smelled of sweat and food and together the three would walk through dusty dirt alleys to Richard's parents basement, plug in their guitars and one microphone into one amplifier and play through their songs. Richard was twenty-one, the Bullfiddler sixteen and Bobby fifteen at the time they met. They rehearsed every day after school and on Saturday and Sunday until 6:30 in the evening so Bobby and the Bullfiddler could make it home for dinner. The rehearsals gave Bullfiddler an appetite and he began to put on a few pounds. Together the three formed their first Texas rock band The Downbeats in 1964.

The Downbeats had business cards made up with three stick figures on the card, two guitar players and a drummer, with Richard, Bobby and Bullfiddlers telephone numbers printed under the stick figures. During this period the three of them would go together to high school dances to check out the local live bands. The best El Paso band at that time 'The Wild Ones' had Bobby Sotello on bass and Ty Grimes on drums swirling his sticks like small batons above his head while keeping a pulsating rhythm. Grimes later literally ran from a draft physical and went on to play drums for Ricky Nelson at Madison Square Garden and on subsequent Nelson recordings.

The Downbeats first audition was at Coronado High School, a tony El Paso west side rich kids school perched on a hill near the western base of Mt. Franklin. The school has a commanding view of El Paso, Mexico and New Mexico. The Downbeats took a cab to the Coronado audition after only three weeks of daily rehearsals. The trio played the five songs they had learned and when the student and faculty judges asked the trio to play more Richard told the committee that The Downbeats would play more if they were hired. The Downbeats failed their audition but continued to rehearse; three months later they had a set list of twenty or so rockers including two instrumentals.

During this time Bobby Parker played fluid licks on a burgundy red solid-body horn shaped Gibson guitar through a Fender Bandmaster piggyback amplifier. The Bullfiddler had been saving some lunch money and after washing cars and mowing lawns was able with Richards gift of gab to put a down payment on a Fender Mustang six-string guitar with a very smooth, thin neck, unlike what Bullfiddler had been used to. He played the Fender through a large heavy Fender Showman piggy-back amplifier. Mrs. Shapiro owned the music store in downtown El Paso and she let The Downbeats take instruments and accessories out of the store on credit with The Downbeats promising and then making small monthly payments. The Downbeats developed good credit and used it to buy one thing or another, a microphone or a stand here, drumsticks and strings there. The Downbeats made their payments regularly. Mrs. Shapiro owned the only music store in downtown El Paso. This was convenient for The Downbeats who still did not have a car.

Chapter 4

EL PASO MUSIC

By 1965 The Downbeats guitars and amps were almost paid off. Richard had deducted the payments from the earnings the trio made at their three or four night a week gigs in downtown El Paso. For a PA Richard and the boys built two matching four foot high plywood speaker cabinets each with a fifteen inch speaker and a horn wired into a single female plug in the back of each of the two cabinets. The Downbeats put coasters on the bottom of each cabinet and handles on the sides for easier moving. Richard took the speaker boxes to Juarez, Mexico and had them upholstered in black tuck-and-roll Naugahyde with a new-car like smell. The black tuck and roll looked sharp and Richard made sure the boxes didn't get scraped or marred in transit. The Juarez upholsters even stapled matching fabric to the front of each box, covering the speakers and horns.

That July three months before Bullfiddler turned seventeen The Downbeats auditioned for and picked up their first regular weekend gig at a bar called the Copacabana on south El Paso street some four blocks from the International bridge to Juarez, Mexico. The Copa was one floor below street level with the stage at the far end of the dimly lit dance floor. The Copa had no windows, smelled of cigarettes and stale beer and had an elevated box next to the stage for the go-go dancers. The bar had lighting from the beer signs hanging haphazardly on the walls all around the bar except for a 'make-out' corner area. The light cut through the heavy smoky haze. There was a dressing-storage room in back of the stage where The Downbeats later stored most of their gear and stage clothes under lock and key. Richard began keeping a fifth of whiskey behind his drum kit during gigs, grudgingly sharing it with the still-underage Bullfiddler and Bobby. Bobby and and the Bullfiddler always took their guitars home after the gigs until The Downbeats began playing for drinks and tips-only in Juarez. Then the guitars stayed in the Copa storeroom.

The Downbeats must have played OK because management at the Copacabana gave the trio a six-month contract as the house band. The Downbeats played every Wednesday, Friday and Saturday night, and on Sunday nights once a month during GI payday. El Paso at that time had a heavy military component with Fort Bliss, Biggs Air Base and White Sands Missile Range. On GI pays both El Paso and Juarez bars were packed with GI's getting as drunk and as loud as possible. There were floor fights often and the Copa's stage was only two feet high off the dance floor. The boys rocked at ground level. One thing those El Paso kids learned early was to avoid the women for fear of alienating a drunk in the bar. As The Downbeats improved as a band they began to attract girls and each one had to eventually talk or fight his way out of scrapes with angry wanna be drunk boyfriends.

    The Downbeats were too busy playing in downtown El Paso to try to get high school gigs which paid well but called for transporting gear. None of The Downbeats had a car, and transported gear by taxi when changing venues. On one occasion The Downbeats did enter a battle of the bands contest held in the gymnasium at Cathedral High School. Cathedral High School is situated half way up a steep hill with a commanding view of El Paso and Juarez from the church side front steps. There were four or five other bands in the contest and their performance was judged by the amount of applause each band received after their set. Downbeats came in second taking home a ribbon and twenty-five dollars in cash. The money went to by 'band supplies'. That night there was also a battle of the drummers and Richard, ever the very hyperactive showman won that contest, beating out the local legend Ty Grimes.

    Bobby and the Bullfiddler will never forget a night before a gig when a lone angry cholo' wanted to fight Bobby because the cholo's girlfriend had shown an interest in Bobby. Together they and a small crowd headed for the alley behind the club. On their way to the back alley one of Los Destroyers a Second Ward Chicano gang confronted Bobby's assailant, knocked him to the ground, put the boot to him. The gang member must have liked The Downbeats music because that Second Ward gang and The Downbeats became good friends. On occasion some of the gang members helped the band carry their gear when The Downbeats played The Goldfinger, another downtown El Paso bar. After their contract expired at the Copa The Downbeats played a three month gig at the San Francisco Private Club and when the Copa offered The Downbeats more money and a longer contract and the band returned to the Copa and played three to four nights a week for the following year.

    The Bullfiddler was making regular money, good for a high school student when you figure what the bar payed the band plus the cash tips the band had to split with two go-go dancers. Even before paying off his guitar, Bullfiddler had money, nice clothes and an active life as things started going badly at Bullfiddlers home. He was developing a rebellious rocker attitude with his late hours and night-life partying ways. Bullfiddler was issued his Social Security card when he turned nine and until he joined the Downbeats he worked every summer in Ruidoso, New Mexico or El Paso as a store clerk, bowling alley pin boy, stable hand, grocery stocker and carnival ride operator. Bullfiddler was now getting paid for playing music. Bullfiddler did not realize Social Security had not been sent in to the IRS for any of those jobs he had in New Mexico and Texas through those early nine years of employment. The employers, now long gone took the monies out of Bullfiddlers checks but failed to send it to the IRS. When playing music, Bullfiddler was always paid cash.

Bullfiddler moved out of his parents home the day he turned seventeen in 1964 and moved in with Richard, sleeping on a sofa next to the drum kit in Richards basement rehearsal room. This was rough because Richard, always hyperactive would come downstairs and play a drum solos while Bullfiddler was sleeping after playing late the night before, or early before Richard went to work and Bullfiddler went to school. Richard could get by on three hours of sleep so it wasn't long before the Bullfiddler rented his first apartment. In 1965 Bullfiddler was the only student in high school to have his own place. By the time Bullfiddler was in his senior hippy year of high school things had changed dramatically. While his friends in high school were talking about having a date with Suzy or Lisa on game night The Downbeats were living with abandon, partying regularly after rehearsals or gigs. School became more and more difficult for Bobby and the Bullfiddler and relating to the El Paso High School social scene was becoming challenging. At the time Bullfiddler was paying one $75.00 a month for his small apartment on Oregon Street in Sunset Heights with electricity included and television on local airwaves was free. During this period Bullfiddler began taking trips on LSD in its original tablet form, Orange Barrels or Purple Micro-Dot and school subjects finally became very interesting and Bullfiddlers attraction to the Rolling Stones grew. In his mind the future bass player saw in the Rolling Stones a band that was not made up of 'pretty boys' like the Beach Boys or Frankie Avalon, or Elvis or the Everly Brothers. The Stones were ugly rough English boys who made it on their rebellious music and grit rather than on looks and perfect harmonies. If the Stones could do this, he thought, anyone could. The LSD tripping lasted off and on for two years before Bullfiddler lost interest, but he vividly remembered the early morning west Texas colorful sunrises from the hills surrounding El Paso or listening to the colorful Beatles White and Magical Mystery Tour albums. The genius of the Beatles lyrics and musicianship combined with the vivid colors of the LSD made Bullfiddler grateful to be alive. Richard, on the other hand drank but never got drunk, smoked pot or did any drugs.

Chapter 5

JUAREZ MUSIC

On New Year's Eve, 1966 Richard booked The Downbeats for a good paying New Year's Eve job playing in a smoke filled Juarez bar, sharing the stage and sets with a Mexican band. While the local Mexican band played Juarez women did their striptease act and when The Downbeats played their set a husky blonde American from New Orleans with rings on every finger performed her routine. The rooms backstage smelled of urine and marijuana. Richard to his credit took care of the immigration questions and paperwork to get The Downbeats instruments, drums and PA equipment over the International downtown bridge to the downtown Juarez bar and back to El Paso.

On that small Juarez stage, the strippers burlesque dancing became progressively more and more risque as the night wore on. When it was twelve o'clock midnight the audience drank up and sang Auld Ang Syne. Everyone in the bar except the band and the bartenders threw their empty glasses against the walls, shattering glass that rained down on everyone in the bar. The Downbeats finished playing around 4:30 am, making it back to El Paso by sunrise to unload their equipment. Young Bullfiddler made it to bed by 7:00 am, slept until two in the afternoon, dressed and went back to Richards basement to set up the gear and have another rehearsal. Bobby was two hours late and took a tongue lashing from Richard.

This is a partial song list of The Downbeats first sets in 1964-67:

    Help . . . . Beatles
    Dizzy Miss Lizzie . . . . Beatles
    Satisfaction . . . Stones
    The Last Time . . . Stones
    Be Bop a Lu La . . . Vincent

As Tears Go By . . . Stones
You Really Got Me . . . Kinks
Its All Over Now . . . Stones
19th Nervous Breakdown . . . Stones
I Fought The Law . . . Fuller
Wolly Bully . . . Sam the Sham and the Pharaohs
Gloria . . . unknown
House of The Rising Sun . . . . Animals
Whole Lotta Shakin' Goin' On . . . Jerry Lee Lewis
Dream . . . . Everly Brothers
I Wanna Hold Your Hand . . . Beatles
I Saw Her Standing There . . . Beatles
Folsom Prison . . . Johnny Cash
Love Me Tender . . . Elvis
I Can't Stop Lovin' You . . . Elvis
Rave On . . . Buddy Holly
You Really Got Me . . . Zombies
I'm a Loser . . . Beatles
Ticket to Ride . . . Beatles
For Your Love . . . Yardbirds
Heart Full of Soul . . . Yardbirds

    The Downbeats with no bass, two guitars and drums quickly learned instrumentals by the Ventures. The trio learned and played 'Pipeline', 'Wipe Out' and 'Walk Don't Run' and 'Perfidia'. 'Wipe Out' was the first instrumental The Downbeats learned on Richard's insistence because the song has numerous drum solos giving Richard a chance to show off his drumming skills. Bobby and the Bullfiddler only sang two songs each night with Richard singing the rest of the three fifteen song sets. Bullfiddler sang lead vocals on 'Dizzy Miss Lizzie' and 'Be Bop a Lula'.

    The set list was 96 percent up-tempo because El Paso bar owners,like bar owners everywhere wanted their crowds to dance and work up a thirst. When there was dancing the bars sold more drinks and the more the crowd drank, the more job security The Downbeats had. The Mod style was popular during that early hippy period so the trio started growing their hair long and wore stylish high collared silk shirts with striped bell-bottomed slacks. The band kept some stage clothes in the dressing room at the Copacabana. Both Bobby and the young Bullfiddler were now getting kicked out of El Paso High School often during their junior and senior years not for bad behavior but for their hair length. It was during this period that the hippy movement reached El Paso, somewhat later than when it arrived in San Francisco and other parts of the country.

There was one exceptional change in teen behavior that stood out during those El Paso hippy years; the bullies, the guys who would get into fights after school at football games and at dances became uncommonly peaceful. While Bullfiddler worked as a part-time clerk in one of El Paso's first head shops on Mesa street adjacent to U.T El Paso, Tony, a well-known high school bully walked in and up to the Bullfiddler. Tony and his brother Paul were hard-core El Paso street fighters who always had a fight with someone after a football game or at a dance. When Tony came up to the counter the nervous Bullfiddler stepped back thinking Tony was going to attack as he had twice in the past.

The last fight Tony and the Bullfiddler had was six months earlier on the dance floor and then outside in back of the Randy Fuller smoke-free teen center. Bobby Fuller by this time had died and Bobby's brother Randy was lost and devastated. A bass player, Randy Fuller opened a short lived teen center in Kern Place on El Paso's west side. When asked one night how the Bobby Fuller Four compared with the Beatles, Randy said: "They are close, but they are not from Texas". It was bass players like Randy Fuller and Bobby Sotello of 'The Wild Ones' that made Bullfiddler wish The Downbeats had a bass player. He could feel the power of the bass all the way to his core.

At the incense laden head shop Tony had a non-threatening way about him and peacefully asked Bullfiddler if he knew where he could buy a $10.00 lid, then an ounce of marijuana. All the bullies Bullfiddler knew became peaceful hippies and for two or three years there was a lull in El Paso teen violence. Some of El Paso's meanest bullies turned hippy later became prominent citizens as adult El Pasoans. The Chicano gangs downtown in El Paso's Second Ward fought for turf, but west, central and north-side El Paso kids saw very little rough stuff.

In 1966 the Vietnam War was taking off and the drinking age in Texas was twenty one. The bars in El Paso closed at midnight so The Downbeats gave last call and stopped playing at 11:45 pm. Richard, with all his energy had an idea that The Downbeats could play in Juarez, and one Friday night after a Copacabana gig the trio went to Juarez and dropped into a bar with a Mexican rock band. The Mexican band played all the latest English language hit cover songs and sang with good harmonies using good English but the Juarez band members themselves memorized the English lyrics and did not speak English. On GI payday weekends the Mexican bands often played until 4:30 or 5:00 am and bilingual Richard managed to talk one of these bands into letting The Downbeats sit in. After The Downbeats played a short five-song set the GIs in the bar bought The Downbeats drinks and gave them tips. This became a regular weekend event for The Downbeats; the Mexican band got a break to eat, smoke foul smelling Mexican cigarettes and have a drink and the soldiers helped Richard, Bobby and the Bullfiddler get drunk and put some cash in their pockets. Eventually Bobby got tired of it all, he had a girlfriend in El Paso and his father was coming down on him for his shoddy schoolwork and his late hours with the band. Bobby was loudly feuding on a daily basis with both Richard and his working class father.

It was during this period that Bullfiddler began to hang out at the Lobby Bar in Juarez where Long John Hunter was the main musical attraction with a strong rhythm and blues act. Long John, a black talented bluesman would jump up from the stage, grab a roof rafter and play excellent lead guitar with one hand while hanging from the rafter with the other hand. Long John was quickly becoming a major influence on young Bullfiddler. One night The Hells Angles from California visited Juarez and crashed some west coast motorcycles through the wall of the Lobby Bar. The Bullfiddler didn't see the event but he read about it in The El Paso Times, El Paso's morning newspaper and saw the hole in the Lobby Bar wall later that night. The Bullfiddler noted that when Long John Hunter sang and played guitar he sang and played like he felt and meant what he was singing about. The young El Pasoan took an opportunity to sit in with Long John years later when Long John began to play around El Paso. On one occasion Bullfiddler played bass on one song while Long John with an extra long guitar chord disappeared into the men's room during the middle of the song. Another musician, John's Oriental understudy walked out of the men's room playing lead guitar. Long John later walked in the front door, sat at the bar and ordered a drink. This showmanship earned Long John a roaring round of applause from all in the bar for that stunt.

Eventually some Austinites discovered Long John, brought him to Austin where he and other Austin musicians recorded two albums produced by Tary Owens. The recordings were done at Gem/Lone Star Studios with Derek O'Brien on guitar, Kaz Kazanoff and Art Lewis playing tenor saxes, Johnny Nicholas on piano, Dave Keown on bass and Kevin Taylor on drums. The producer took lucrative songwriting credit along with Hunter on six of the songs on the Bordertown Legend Album and five songwriting co-credits on Long John's 'Ride With Me' album. Long John Hunter then played a few shows at Austin's Continental Club, Antones and the Victory Bar and Grill in east Austin before returning to El Paso to play more hometown gigs. He occasionally toured Europe and received an occasional royalty check in the mail for his Austin-made recordings.

Chapter 6

THE BUST

In 1968 Bullfiddler was arrested in his apartment and charged with growing and possessing s small amount of marijuana. He had small pie tins with budding two inch high plants and part of a ten dollar lid sitting on his dresser. Bullfiddler's father who wrote for the El Paso Times daily newspaper had just written a three-part article on the new 'hippy movement' in El Paso. The El Paso Times editor saw to it that the story of the young musicians bust was featured right next to the first of the series Bullfiddlers father had written. The editor justified running the two stories side by side to demonstrate that there was no editorial favoritism on the newspaper and that the 'hippy problem' was real in El Paso.

The write-up appeared on the front page of The El Paso Times and on the Metro Section of the evening El Paso Herald Post. The announcement caused Bullfiddler's Jewish family a lot of humiliation. The Jewish temple in El Paso relayed to the boys family that Bullfiddler was not welcome in the Temple; he was deemed a bad influence. Bullfiddlers father refused to bail Bullfiddler out of the El Paso County Jail, letting him sit there for almost three months before Bullfiddler made bail. He did this in the hopes of frightening Bullfiddler into cleaning up his act. Bullfiddler's father was also a lawyer. He declined to represent Bullfiddler in court thinking that he did not want to enable the boy. Bullfiddler hired Lee Chagra, then a locally famous criminal attorney with a good record of getting favorable treatment for those busted for drugs. Because of Lee Chagra Bullfiddler was given a differed adjudication with the understanding that the charges would be dropped if he stayed out of trouble for three years and reported to his probation officer monthly. After the three years the charges were dropped and Bullfiddler was able to eventually become a certified Texas school teacher.

Lee Chagra was killed in his new law office on Mesa Street, two houses down from El Paso's Cathedral where the funeral was held. Lee's brothers Jimmy and Joe later hired Woody Harrilson's father to kill Judge Wood in San Antonio. The judge was killed and the two Chagra brothers and Charles Harrelson were sentenced to federal time in Leavenworth. Both the Chagra brothers and Bullfiddler were graduates of El Paso High School with only a few years separating each other.

El Paso High School as with the Jewish Temple did not want Bullfiddler around so Bullfiddler, a senior when busted took classes on Mondays, Wednesdays and Fridays at the El Paso Independent School District main offices. El Paso High School later sent Bullfiddler his diploma in the mail minus a commencement invitation. Bullfiddler had argued successfully with the El Paso School District Superintendent that he was being deprived of his high school diploma while in his senior year and was being punished before his case was adjudicated, contrary to what the El Paso School system had been teaching about being 'innocent until proven guilty'. The El Paso Independent School District Superintendent set up the three-day-a week tutorial at the Administration building some three blocks from Bullfiddlers apartment.

Bullfiddler was now known around El Paso not for his musical activities but for his drug bust and his association with Lee Chagra. This gave the teenager a lot to talk about until he entered college at UTEP where he never mentioned the episode.

Chapter 7

A SMUGGLING MOMMA

Bulllfiddlers mother liked to drink liquor and she would buy and import Juarez liquor, lots of it. During the 1960's American Immigration would only let adults bring back two bottles per person so she stuffed bottles under the front seat and the three grade schoolers were told not to say anything to Immigration about the booze hidden under the seat. When the young family crossed the border back into the United States the kids were only allowed to only tell Immigration officers their citizenship. 'American!', they yelled while Bullfiddler's mother declared 'groceries, two bottles of liquor and two haircuts, forgetting to mention her prescription and non-prescription drugs and the rest of the hidden liquor. The customs agent would then direct the young mother to drive over to station #6 where she would pay the tax on the two bottles of liquor. When they reached their west side El Paso home Bullfiddlers mother unloaded the booze while the siblings carried in the groceries. It was common for some neighbors to be in the smuggling business and their maids worked illegally for thirteen to fifteen dollars a week (plus room and board). International shopping was heavy in El Paso in the 1960's and by the time Bullfiddler reached high school he could speak basic street Spanish.

Years later Bullfiddler's first marriage in 1971 was to a well-traveled military dependent he met during his freshman year in college. He quickly noticed the sweet coconut smell about her. They were married for seven years and she never knew Bullfiddler was a musician because they had no musical instruments in any of their apartments or homes. They were 'serious' students. In 1976 Mr. and Mrs. Bullfiddler bought a house in the green lush Upper Valley in far west El Paso. By this time Bullfiddler was teaching in New Mexico and he and his wife were in graduate school at UTEP. Bullfiddler still did not have a guitar but he did have a Harley Davidson motorcycle he traded a Triumph Bonneville in for. Bullfiddler made numerous bike runs to the Aspencade in Ruidoso, New Mexico in late September when the aspen trees changed color. He set up camp creek-side on the Mescalaro Indian Reservation, drank in the Buckaroo Bar with all the bikers and returned to El Paso as part of a Texas Bandito run.

The music in the Buckaroo Bar was uninhibited but seemed to Bullfiddler to lack polish with their starts, the way the band ended their songs and the lack of dynamics, but their very loud, floor-shaking free spirit moved Bullfiddler to keep coming back to that bar once a year for three years. The experience made him finally miss working with The Downbeats. His wife never went with him on these runs, she was falling in love with a man who owned a gift shop on St. Thomas Island. One day Bullfiddlers well-traveled wife awoke to the fact that she was chained to a thirty-year mortgage in El Paso and after having traveled around a good part of the world, El Paso had lost it's romantic attraction.

The Bullfiddler and his wife tried the same smuggling stunt his mother practiced. When they were undergraduates in 1973 at UTEP the Bullfiddler and his first ex-wife threw a party for an English class the two took together. Unfortunately the sniffing customs agent looked under the front seat of the same beat-up Ford station wagon his mother had given the couple on their wedding. The long-haired Bullfiddler and his hippy looking wife were found out. The Feds levied a fine of only forty dollars on the students and the Bullfiddler paid it to customs at the bridge. Bullfiddler and his embarrassed wife could have been arrested and booked in the El Paso County Jail on federal charges but the Immigration officers must have had bigger fish to catch because they let the students off with the fine and a warning and the incident was not recorded as an arrest. During this period Disco was very popular in crowded El Paso and Juarez bars and the Bullfiddler had been out of the music performing business for three or four years. He sold his guitars and amps when entering college and did not have a guitar all through undergraduate school. He would would have nothing to do with the 'plastic' Disco, the leisure suits or the music. After surviving the El Paso hippy scene, Disco seemed to Bullfiddler to be ultra commercial and void of any depth. Bullfiddler and his wife divorced in 1977 and Bullfiddler's X never knew Bullfiddler could play guitar and sing numerous songs, not that it would have made a difference in their marriage.

By 1965 Richard was now firmly managing The Downbeats. He still allowed Bobby and the Bullfiddler to sing only two songs each the entire night while he sang lead vocals on all the rest of the songs while playing drums. Bobby and Bullfiddler sang backing vocals and played their guitars. The Downbeats never did hire a bass player but they let a few sit and play for free for brief periods. The singing was becoming a point of contention between Bobby and Richard and they began to argue often.

The one song the Bullfiddler sang well was 'Dizzy Miss Lizzie', the Beatles version. The Bullfiddler played lead guitar on that rocker and when the band went into that song or 'Be Bop a Lula' the crowd packed the dance floor. The reception and reaction those songs had from the crowd upset the ego maniacal Richard. By now the Bullfiddler knew that he could sing but had no desire to push the issue. The Downbeats never recorded anything, they had no reviews of any kind, not one writeup or any listings in the entertainment sections of the either the El Paso Times or the El Paso Herald Post. The entertainment editors were not interested in the 'entertainment' found in downtown El Paso bars and would rather review ballet at UT El Paso than hang with a bunch of sweaty GI's in a cellar bar three blocks from Juarez. Neither of the two newspapers in El Paso ever reviewed the bullfights in the two Juarez corridas either. The Juarez newspapers, El Fronterizo and El Continental always reviewed bullfights along with photos and matador interviews. Quero Rivera and Alfredo Leal were famous matadors in Mexico, well known for their bullkilling expertise. Mexican newspapers often reviewed the local Juarez bar bands while The Downbeats were well known to a hand full of drunk Vietnam bound GIs.

It was much different when the Bullfiddler moved to Austin, Texas where every band he knew or worked with was into recording, band photos, write-ups, posters, demos and even bumper stickers. The Downbeats had none of that but they were a true working bar band nonetheless for almost three years.

An El Paso Beach Boys concert story demonstrates Richards callousness. One night the Beach Boys came to play in the El Paso Sun Bowl. Bobby and Bullfiddler bought tickets while Richard climbed in over a wall to the show. The Downbeats hooked up and watched as the Beach Boys road into the stadium on the back of El Paso Police motorcycles driven by EPPD officers. Occasionally, while the Beach Boys were performing the bands drummer tossed out drumsticks to the crowd for souvenirs, risking putting someone's eye out. One man caught one of the drumsticks and gave it to his small son. As The Downbeats were walking out of the Sun Bowl after the concert, Richard told his bandmates to meet him at his basement. Richard took off running for the gate. As Richard passed the small boy he snatched the drumstick out of the boys hand and ran home. The drumstick sat on a bookshelf in the rehearsal basement until the day The Downbeats broke up. Richard never had any capacity for any empathy or compassion.

It was during 'The Downbeats' heyday that Bullfiddler had a vivid dream about the Rolling Stones. He imagined the Stones were scheduled to play a concert in El Paso and at the last minute Bill Wyman, the Stones bass player became ill. The Stones put out a request for a local stand-in bass player and in that dream Bullfiddler answered the request, played the concert with the Stones at the El Paso County Coliseum and became a local El Paso hero. That dream never came true in that form, but a brief association with the Stones did happen years later in Austin, Texas.

The day The Downbeats broke up Bobby had an argument during rehearsal with Richard over a new schedule and Richard slugged Bobby in the face.

Furious over the assault Bobby announced that he was quitting The Downbeats rather than fight a losing battle with the muscular Italian. Bobby began packing up his guitar while Richard went upstairs. Bobby was mad and humiliated having endured constant arguing. The more gigs The Downbeats played the more the bullying occurred at rehearsals and during performances. Before he left Bobby grabbed the Beach Boys drumstick Richard had stolen from that child at the Beach Boys Sun Bowl concert, broke it into pieces and threw it in a trash can in the dusty alley. Bullfiddler was also glad the gig came to an end.

James Brown came to El Paso in 1967 with his band 'The Flames'. Brown played at the El Paso County Coliseum where Johnny Cash played a year earlier. Cash played his show to a small floor only crowd while James Brown played to a packed room. The Bullfiddler was able to get a back stage pass to the Johnny Cash show from a friend who traded a back stage pass for some pot she said she was scoring for Cash's band. Sure enough while standing stage left at the Coliseum enjoying the Carter family Johnny Cash walked up and stood next to the Bullfiddler. Cash was holding his guitar and the two said nothing to each other. That night Cash gave El Paso a good show. It is interesting to note that in first El Paso show 1966 all the ground level chairs were taken at the Johnny Cash show and all the seats in the upper areas were vacant. In 1973 Johnny Cash again played the El Paso County Coliseum and the entire arena was packed from top to bottom.

Shortly after the Johnny Cash show a friend had two James Brown tickets and asked Bullfiddler if he would like to go to the concert. That afternoon DJ Steve Crosno was interviewing James Brown live at the KELP radio studio located out in the desert near Executive Center in the desert of west El Paso. Bullfiddler and a friend drove out to the KELP studio which was surrounded located not more than two miles from the Mexican and New Mexico borders. A crowd had collected outside the studio door waiting for a glimpse of James Brown who was being interviewed by Crosno on Crosno's Hop, a televised dance show patterned after Dick Clark's American Bandstand. Eventually the station manager came out of the station, got the crowds attention and pointed to a security guard standing alone out in the desert amid the sand dunes and yucca cactus. The guard had four tickets to the show that night the manager announced, and the first four to reach the guard would get the free comps. The mass of crazed El Paso teenagers rushed off toward the lone security guard. James Brown and Steve Crosno sprinted out out of the radio station front door, jumped into a pink Mustang convertible and sped off.

The Bullfiddler saw James Brown and the Flames show that night and was blown away by the energy and precision of the show. He felt apprehensive about going to a 'black' gig, but once Brown and the Fabulous Flames started playing all misconceptions vanished. The coliseum was overflowing and at the end of the show everyone was smiling, hyped and very happy. There had been nothing like the musical power of James Brown in El Paso that Bullfiddler could remember but after Brown there followed a number of other bands, all playing the El Paso County Coliseum, the only venue in town that could hold thousands of people.

Jefferson Airplane (Jefferson Starship) with a pregnant Grace Slick played at the El Paso County Coliseum one night with Papa John Creech playing an old fiddle. Before the concert was over word got out that some of Jefferson Airplane were going to jam in a hippy bar called The Frijolie in Anapra New Mexico. Kids jumped into their cars as soon as the show was over and sped to Anapra, a small New Mexican town on a nipple of New Mexican land that pokes into western El Paso County. The Bullfiddler made it into the bar as the doors were closed and locked. The band with the elderly Papa John Creech minus pregnant Grace Slick jammed until 4 am.

The New Mexico hippy club, 'The Frijolie' was a few blocks from Rosa's Cantina, presumed to be the cantina Marty Robbins wrote about in his song 'El Paso'. Rosa's Cantina is on Doniphan Drive under the shadow of Mt. Christo Rey. Mount Christo Rey has a dirt trail winding around the mountain and tourists and religious pilgramagers would hike to the top of Christo Rey to be close to a statue of Jesus and take in the wonderful view of Texas, Mexico and New Mexico. The mountain is right on the border with Mexico and often Mexican banditos would hold up tourists and flee with their booty back to Mexico. The banditos were also known to occasionally rob a tourist passenger train that weaved through that part of western El Paso County and southern New Mexico. While this was going on Rosa's Cantina hired Spanish language groups play the small room that looked no different than any other bar in the area. Rosas Cantina is now remodeled into a classy upscale restaurant but in the 1960's it was a shoddy beer and wine juke joint.

For some reason the Bullfiddler lost the desire to play music after The Downbeats broke up. He had enough of the demands of those long stints gigging in those south El Paso bars, the intense rehearsing and rowdy Juarez scene. College loomed and Bullfiddler gladly let school take take priority over music. The closest he came to music was as a music/movie critic for the UTEP campus student newspaper, The Prospector occasionally sitting in now on bass with Long John Hunter. One of his college friends had an electric bass guitar and he let Bullfiddler once play around with it. The neck was longer than his old Fender Mustang guitar and Bullfiddler was so intrigued that while in graduate school he bought his first electric bass guitar, a Hofner copy viola-shaped lightweight hollow body bass with a short neck. The Bullfiddler must have thought he was going to be another Paul McCartney and by the time Bullfiddler reached graduate school he felt it would be more exciting and easier to play that strong deep bass drive than a six string guitar. After all the bass had only four strings, how hard could it be? The Bullfiddler knew he would never be any good as a lead guitarist even though he had some good licks with The Downbeats. By 1976 Bullfiddler began a life long love affair for the deep powerful rumbling sound of the bass guitar and later on the acoustic bullfiddle. Before he moved permanently to Austin the Bullfiddler did some traveling starting with the Peace Corps.

Chapter 8

ESCAPING EL PASO

    Bullfiddler played guitar briefly during a stint in the Peace Corps in North Yemen in 1979. While studying Arabic in Rowdah, a small primitive community northwest of Sana'a, he borrowed a guitar from a fellow PCV and played and sang for Yemenis at the local dusty souk with a strong coffee smell. Bullfiddler saw firsthand how prevalent music piracy is world-wide. At the souk a music store had a wide collection of music of all kinds from all over the world. The Bullfiddler bought his first tape, a Johnny Cash collection and watched as the proprietor put a master tape in a tape machine, a blank in another machine and high speed dubbed the original onto the blank cassette copy. Before he was done with his Peace Corps tour Bullfiddler had amassed a wide music collection, all bootleg and had later had no problem bringing the music back to Texas. The climate in North Yemen was identical to the climate in El Paso. It was desert, hot, dry and windy and with even fewer trees. He was by now used to having neither a television or a telephone.
    The Bullfiddlers guitar playing and singing for the Yemeni was far from spectacular, but one night during the Islamic holiday Ramadan, Bullfiddler was playing and singing a Hank Williams song in between reviewing flash cards for his studies in Arabic when some dogs began to fight across the dirt lot from the small souk. One of the Yemeni domino players, hungry and edgy took his AK 47 and fired a few loud shots into the pack of wild dogs to run them off, leaving the smell of cordite heavy in the air of the souk. The Bullfiddler walked home later that night past one dead dog, its legs up in the air, leaning against the wall. It had been cut almost in half by a burst from the Yemeni's Russian assault rifle. The remains of the dog were gone the next day, when the wild dog scavengers finished their nightly prowl on Rowdahs dirt covered streets. There

is no garbage pick up in Yemen. The dogs nightly pick the streets clean. That night was the last time the Bullfiddler played guitar in North Yemen.

After returning to El Paso from his Peace Corps stint Bullfiddler took his electric bass to England, thinking he could land a gig. The Bullfiddler lived in England for nine months and never joined a band or even jammed with anyone, realizing that if he had an amplifier or an acoustic bass or talent he could have found opportunities to play music in England. While living in HyWycomb Bullfiddler read in 'Stone Alone' that Bill Wyman got his gig with the Stones because he had a huge amplifier and in their beginning the Stones ran vocals, guitar and bass from that one amp of Wymans. Once again Bullfiddler wasn't thinking things through.

While working in England for the American Department of Defense Bullfiddler heard the story of how some American military and state department kids found fame with Apple Records with their rock group 'America'. These kids were students at London Central High School in Hy Wycombe where Bullfiddler worked as a high school counselor for the Department of Defense. These teenagers formed the band 'America' at the high school and practiced in the school cafeteria after class. After a few months of writing and jamming together 'America' started taking the train to London on Fridays after school and would came back to London Central High School on the last train, missing the school curfew and were put on restriction for two weeks. When the kids got off restriction they went back to London again, this time spending the entire weekend. They were put on restriction often. This pattern went on until the band returned to London, spent a week there and came back to school with a recording contract with the Beatles Apple Records. The Bullfiddler admired their chutzpah and wished he had some.

Bullfiddler lugged that bass around England for nine months while working various jobs and only played music along with music from his Yemini made cassettes. He played quietly to himself while developing a love for the smell and taste for thick slabs of juicy English bacon. When he returned stateside immigration searched his baggage thoroughly, thinking he was an actual musician. During the period following his experience in England the Bullfiddler continued playing along with his music and by the time Bullfiddler reached Austin, Texas he could play bass to all Elvis Presley and Roy Orbison songs as well most of the older rockers. The Bullfiddler was not at that time a Country and Western fan so it was either an ironic accident or divine intervention that he landed his first band job in Austin with a hard core country and western band, 'Debbie Norrad and Pure Country', but before Bullfiddler moved to Austin he still had a travel bug and found work briefly in Central America. This time he left his bass at his parents home.

While teaching English in Costa Rica in 1980, Bullfiddler discovered a musicians mildew covered bar across the street from a large church and catty corner from the main plaza in the central part of downtown San Jose. The bar was frequented by musicians but there was never any live music. The bar had a lone telephone on the wall and when it rang someone answered it and turned the telephone over to the one of the band members. The caller most often wanted live music for a party and the Costa Rican band leader would jot down the address of the party, motion to 'the boys' and the band all climbed into a van parked out front, went and played the party and then returned to the bar to await the call for their next gig. Three or four Costa Rican bands operated out of the bar. One musician did go out to his van, retrieve a guitar and let Bullfiddler play a few songs. The guys were polite but unimpressed. One small eleven year old boy, hung out at the bar running errands for the musicians. Later in Panama city with the smell of diesel everywhere, while watching a blind old fiddler playing to a downtown crowd the Bullfiddler spotted the kid who apparently roamed Central America at will, at his young age. The borders in Central America were very easy for undocumented people to navigate and Bullfiddler was amazed that such a small child could travel from one country to another with such ease. Bullfiddler returned to El Paso with its refinery generated sulfur smells by way of Panama in 1980 having finally lost his desire to travel.

 A few weeks before Bullfiddler left El Paso for Austin, the western swing band 'Asleep at the Wheel' played at The New Buffalo Bar in El Paso. The Bullfiddler saw that exciting band with an upright bass player standing and playing at the piano players left. Together the piano and bullfiddle set out a strong bottom in conjunction with a horn and fiddle player. All the band members except the drummer had to duck when band leader Ray Benson swing the microphone with an extended cable over the band members heads. Benson has great showmanship as did each of his superb musicians. The band had timing and rhythm that was impeccable and it made the Bullfiddler and other El Pasoans want to dance.

 The closest Bullfiddler came to a recording studio in El Paso was in 1972 when Bullfiddler sold a review of the opening of El Adobe Recording Studio on El Paso Drive to the El Paso Times. El Adobe, Bullfiddler noted, was an expensive set-up in a south central building built in 1928. Lynyrd Skynyrd was the first group to record at the El Adobe Studio and the band as well as other celebrities were at the opening night party. Bullfiddler noted that the studio was designed by Howard Steel, director of Studio 55 in Hollywood. Tye Grimes, currently drumming for Ricky Nelson was at the party as was Jimmy Carl Black who was working with Frank Zappa. The El Adobe had various rates in 1979. They featured $80.00 an hour for 24 tracks, $60.00 an hour for 16 tracks and $25.00 an hour for two tracks.

 El Adobe had three open houses parties actually, one for musicians, one for the press and one for Christian musicians interested in recording for their church. Sonny and the Mesilla Valley Lowboys were recording the night of the press party and Bullfiddler could see the musicians working through the large window separating the control room from the musicians. The sound in the control room headphones was in Bullfiddlers opinion excellent. The Lowboys finished their recording two weeks later and sent the tape for pressing to somebody in Bakersfield California. The studio failed by the time Bullfiddler made it to Austin in 1982.

Two months before Bullfiddler left El Paso for Austin he met Cecil Hart at The Chamizal Theater. The Theater sat some 300 yards from Juarez, Mexico and was near and named after the only land the United States ever gave away to a foreign country. President Kennedy gave some Chamizal land to Mexico after a prolonged debate in Washington about the Rio Grande's pre-levee history of changing its path often when it rained hard. Washington and Kennedy concluded that the acres should be returned to Mexico complete with all structures. Cecil Hart was playing cow bones that night at the Chamizal Theater during a statewide fiddle contest. Cecil's rhythms were so impressive that Bullfiddler was excited to meet and write a review of Cecil, 66 and his performance. Cecil had been playing the same bones since 1928. Using two cow rib bones in each hand Cecil was able to perform various snappy rhythms with pizazz.

When Bullfiddler arrived in Austin in 1982 'Asleep at the Wheel' was fresh in Bullfiddlers mind. The band was playing a free concert at Auditorium Shores on a Wednesday night and Bullfiddler went to his first free Austin concert. He had no trouble siding up to the right side of the stage and stayed there the entire show which unlike El Paso, was free. The show would be Bullfiddlers introduction to the free quality music there was and still is in Austin and there were beautiful women everywhere.

Bullfiddler would find a number of places where he would see and hear quality music in Austin for free. Threadgills on North Lamar Boulevard was the club nearest to where Bullfiddler worked on his first job in Austin. Threadgills allowed people to listen to good musicians in an informal setting without charging a cover. Some of these Austin musicians Bullfiddler noted, were often featured in The New Yorker Magazine's 'Goings On About Town' section; many Threadgills musicians had just come back or were booked to go on European, Oriental or South American tours. They all seemed to enjoy playing for their home crowd.

REJECTION

The Bullfiddlers day jobs in El Paso before relocating to Austin was as a freelance writer for various El Paso publications and law clerking with an old high school buddy who had a law practice and was also a local El Paso city councilman. The law office job led Bullfiddler to work temporarily as a campaign manager for another lawyer friend who was running for District Clerk in El

Paso. Both lawyers lost their respective political races and the Bullfiddler was half heartedly studying the LSAT manual with the aim of going to law school. Since he had two degrees and nine months clerking in a law office Bullfiddler mistakenly believed he could get into law school. He took the LSAT without really studying for the exam and was rejected by the four law schools he applied to. On a whim, Bullfiddler left El Paso in a Honda Civic with his Hofner bass and attempted to talk the admissions directors of the four law schools (San Antonio, Houston, Oklahoma City and Lubbock) into letting Bullfiddler enroll on scholastic probation. Some of the school admission directors gently laughed and others told the lawyer wannabe to retake the LSAT, raise his score by three points and reapply.

The Bullfiddler found himself alone in Lubbock, Texas rejected, dejected and downhearted and not wanting to return to El Paso a failure. He took a job as a bartender in Lubbock where he met C.B. Stubbefield, a proud man who owned a strong mesquite smelling barbecue joint on Broadway street just east of the railroad tracks. This was a musical eye opener for the Bullfiddler and Mr. Stubbefield and he would meet again and become good friends in Austin. Stubbs, as he was affectionately known relocated to Austin the same year Bullfiddler did and eventually let Bullfiddler and his friend Curley host an open mic at his BBQ joint on North Central I-35 near downtown Austin.

Chapter 9

AUSTIN TEXAS

After tending bar in Lubbock for a few weeks the Bullfiddler drove into Austin, Texas and took two part-time jobs, as a prep cook at the Stallion Restaurant on North Lamar Blvd., and a part-time clerk in Dan's Liquor Store on Burnett Street. It didn't take the Bullfiddler long to decide to 'put it down' in Austin, Texas. Almost immediately while wandering Barton Springs Bullfiddler realized that unlike El Paso, he would never starve with all the thousands of pecans lying everywhere and the waters of Barton Springs made him realize that he would never die of thirst. The air was clean with no sulfur or auto fumes in the air. Water and jobs were scarce in El Paso and when Bullfiddler arrived in Austin in 1982 he found that anyone who wanted to work could work, pay rent, eat, go to school and have an social life. El Paso was dry and dusty dirty year round while Austin was always very green and lush. South Austin reminded Bullfiddler of the carefree uninhibited hippies days in El Paso. The citizens of Austin were an attractive group and very friendly. Bullfiddler made up his mind to find a job and took one at The Stallion Restaurant on North Lamar his second day in town. Had Bullfiddler been job hunting in El Paso, with thirteen percent unemployment he might have to wait weeks before getting a job.

Daily, when mopping the floor at The Stallion Bullfiddler would first put a dollar in the juke box and play Joe Ely's 'I Grow My Fingernails Long So They Click when I Play the Piano' and then mop with gusto to the rhythms of the song. A few months later the restaurant closed the day before Thanksgiving but by then Bullfiddler had another part-time job selling liquor at Dan's Liquor Store on Burnett.

Slowly at first Bullfiddler began to experience the wide variety of music lifestyles that went with the musicianship found in countless Austin bars and cafes. Live and especially original music was rare and hard to find in El Paso while in Austin he heard various types of music while walking down the streets. The music not only came from businesses but from homes and apartments as well. It was everywhere.

There was no dust anywhere in Austin and there were many Hispanics in Austin but not as many as the 73 percent of the population of El Paso. Bullfiddler noticed quickly that when he spoke Spanish to a Hispanic in Austin they almost always replied in English. This reminded Bullfiddler of his experience in Fort Worth where it seemed as if the further one moved away from the border with Mexico, the more insistent Hispanics were on trying to assimilate into American society. When Bullfiddler arrived in Austin he was six feet tall and weighed one hundred and seventy pounds. He was also losing his hair.

Bullfiddlers first musical experience as a player in Austin occurred when he sat in on electric bass with Joe Valentine while Valentine's bass playing brother took a break and a break. Bullfiddler found the courage to ask and be allowed to sit in on bass guitar at the Shorthorn Lounge with the Supernatural Family Band. Bullfiddler had no qualms now about asking to sit in on bass. Playing bass in front of strangers was now exciting. While eating lunch next door to Dan's Liquor store at a small Mexican restaurant that smelled a lot like Juarez, Bullfiddler talked with a woman who told him about a country and western band that was auditioning for a bass player. The Bullfiddler asked for the band's telephone number, called the band and set up an audition for a Friday night at a bar on highway 71 near Bergstrom Airport.

By eight pm. that Friday night 'Debbie Norrad and Pure Country' was in full stride. A large bearded man, Debbie's husband saw Bullfiddler with his caseless Beatle bass enter the bar and invited him to sit at a table next to the jukebox. George Norrad had a half gallon of Jim Beam and offered the Bullfiddler a drink which he gladly accepted, slugging it down in one or two gulps. On stage Debbie was playing country standards for a sweating smoking, working men's crowd. Her bass player was an older man who wore a sailors hat and played a red and white Fender Squire Bass. Bullfiddler noticed that the old bassman plucked the thick strings with his thumb. Debbie quickly invited the Bullfiddler on stage whereupon the old bassman took off the Fender and handed it to Bullfiddler. After three songs, Debbie turned toward the Bullfiddler and told him the job was his if he wanted it. Bullfiddler had his first Austin musician job and he gladly played hard core country and western the rest of the night.

Something happened that night that has never happened again in the Bullfiddlers music career. There was a bar fight-riot that broke out on the dance floor while he and Debbie Norrad and Pure Country were playing their third and last set. During the fistfight the band did not miss a beat, and George, Debbie's six-foot four three-hundred-plus pound husband stood between the band and the fighters, occasionally pushing the rowdies back into the crowd. George never hit anyone but by the end of the night Bullfiddlers adrenalin was pumping as though he had just run a foot race. Bullfiddler was paid $30 that night and went back to Austin with a schedule of where they were going to play the rest of that month. Debbie Norrad never called a rehearsal and the band played country standards that were quickly becoming second nature to the Bullfiddler.

Bullfiddler noticed that while playing with Debbie the dancers often choreographed their dancing to the bass runs. Bullfiddler noticed that when he slipped from a 2/4 time to a bass run or walk, the dancers adapted. He had some control over the audience.

Debbie Norrad never played at The Austin Outhouse, but the Bullfiddler first discovered the Outhouse on 32nd & 1/2 and Guadalupe Street The Outhouse had some of the best live entertainment in North Austin at the time. The bar had a South Austin vibe and was located within walking distance from Bullfiddlers one room studio apartment. The bar smelled of beer from the large pitchers, cigarette smoke and pool chalk dust. It did not smell like its namesake but during the summer there were gnats in the Outhouse bathroom. The Outhouse was managed by three great guys, Chuck, Howie and Ed. The bar had an open mic on Tuesday nights and the Outhouse became a regular Bullfiddler hangout and spent a lot of time in the bars backyard with wooded picnic tables full of carved names. The backyard was surrounded by a tall wooden rough unsanded wood fence and musicians and patrons would take their beers and instruments and sit back there awaiting their turn to play their set for the open mic. Sometimes the musicians rehearsed their set, sometimes they recruited other musicians and often they smoked joints. There was always lots of laughter and dancing around the Outhouse mascot, a large calm and quiet dog that hung out at the bar every night. There were times when a band would be loudly rockin' and that dog would be curled up on the dance floor directly in front of the band, at peace with itself regardless of the bands volume.

Bullfiddler watched the Asylum Street Spanker's form and rehearse their show at the Outhouse on Wednesday nights. At first the Spanker's had a small crowd, but within two months they had people lined up outside and watching from the outdoor wings when the stage door was left open. The Spanker's, the Bullfiddler thought, were extremely entertaining with their vaudevillian humor, 1920's costumes and their nonelectrical acoustic music. From those gigs at the Outhouse, the Spanker's toured the world and have acquired a large following in Japan. Stanley Smith the clarinet player was an original Spanker who later played clarinet with Bullfiddler and Boomer Norman as 'Los Downbeats' when Los Downbeats gigged at the Hyde Park Tour of Homes. Stanley, Whammo and Guy Forsythe were founding members of the Spankers and showed that a band could combine music with theater antics and humor.

Debbie Norrad and Pure Country' kept the Bullfiddler busy for over a year. The band played in almost every honky tonk in Bastrop, Elgin, Smithville, LaGrange, Victoria and of course that joint near Bergstrom Airbase where the

Bullfiddler passed his first audition. Once again the band never had any band photos, write-ups, posters MySpace or a Web site. Debbies band worked one or two gigs a week. The band had a guitar player, Jim Parish who had a large hump on his back and an alcoholic overweight girlfriend who came with him to everyone of Debbie's gigs. The band soon lost its drummer so Debbie auditioned drummers at gigs and all of them wanted more money than the Debbie could afford. Debbie was separating from her husband, George who loved her deeply and had paid for her piano and PA system. Eventually Debbie fell in with a drummer and within two weeks Bullfiddler was fired from the band. Debbie's new boyfriend wanted to hire an old pal of his to play bass. Bullfiddler's first experience at getting fired from a band came after a gig at an American Legion hall in the Smithville area.

On one of Bullfiddlers last band jobs with Debbie was in Manor, Texas and The Bullfiddler drove back to Austin with a girlfriend of Debbie's. When the two reached her apartment in East Austin the heavily intoxicated woman couldn't find her keys, she had lost them when she drunkenly fell into a trash pile in back of the bar while she and some of the band stepped out back during a break. She had tripped and fallen into a pile of rancid smelling bar trash, losing her keys in the process. Together the woman and Bullfiddler drove back to Manor where they searched the trash pile and found her keys. It was a tough time for that girl because she and Bullfiddler had to be at work at eight sharp that following morning. They arrived back at her apartment during sunrise just in time to shower off the grime and go to work.

During Bullfiddlers tenure (1982-3) with 'Debbie Norrad and Pure Country' Debbie had talked him into buying her red and white Fender Squire Bullet bass. She asked Bullfiddler to play that bass after the audition thinking that the Hofner Beatle bass was not appropriate for a country band. Bullfiddler bought that bass on the installment plan from Debbie. In 1983 he sold the Beatle bass through Walter Hutchinson's Musical Exchange in Austin and began taking upright acoustic bass lessons at UT's music school. The music school applied double bass instructor, Dr. Neubert let Bullfiddler borrow his first bullfiddle, an old plywood Kay with a warped neck, metal strings that sat high off the wavy uneven fretboard. Bullfiddler changed out the bridge thus lowering the action of the four strings. Bullfiddler played that bullfiddle for two years. Bullfiddler became interested in the bullfiddle because he quickly realized he wasn't a very good bass player and if he wanted work he had to have and be able to play an upright bass. Bullfiddles were rare and expensive at that time. Today the instrument is plentiful but still expensive compared to an electric four-string bass guitar. Bullfiddlers logic worked and soon he began his oddesy of playing behind strangers at open mics that were like musical beehives scattered all over Austin. Bullfiddler was growing accustomed to being a backup bass player and had no interest in running his own band.

Later on Bullfiddler did reconfigure The Downbeats as Los Downbeats, for special occasions like the Hyde Park Tour of Homes gigs or for performances in the mental health field, but Bullfiddler was the only original El Paso Downbeats member. Bullfiddlers had no desire to form a band because he realized how much work would be involved and fronting a band would detract from his day job. Rent and groceries had to come first. One morning while 'Asleep at the Wheel's founder Ray Benson was on Austin local radios the Sam and Bob talk show, Bullfiddler called in, spoke to Ray Benson and asked him what the key was to running a successful band. By that time 'Asleep at the Wheel' had four Grammys to their credit. Ray told the Bullfiddler over the air that the band was the first thing on his mind when he woke up in the morning and the last thing on his mind before he fell asleep. The Bullfiddler was aware of the time commitment at that time and just didn't want to make the commitment. He was enjoying and finding a lot of satisfaction playing pick-up gigs.

Chapter 10

A TEXAS MUSIC SCHOOL

The Bullfiddler signed up for and studied double bass (standup, acoustic, bullfiddle) with Dr. Neubert for two semesters at the University of Texas music school in 1984. Bullfiddler was by now a veteran of one Austin band and he was actively playing in a duet with Tony Brassatt. The textbook Dr. Neubert used at the UT music department for these one-on-one studies was written by Samandl and was written half in English and half in German. In two semesters of one-on-one study with Dr. Nubert Bullfiddler never got passed page nine in the music textbook. He was too lazy to practice scales and assignments at home. During his 'studies' at UT Bullfiddler had a day job and was playing out regularly at night, often four to five nights a week. Out of the kindness of Dr. Nubert's heart he gave Bullfiddler a 'B' each semester, but as a former teacher Bullfiddler realized he deserved a 'D' for the work he did while taking those two classes.

Bullfiddler would later often see Dr. Nubert perform with the Austin Symphony as the head of the Austin Symphony's double bass section. The Austin Symphony delighted Bullfiddler because the Symphony is one of only a few musical groups in Austin with more than one bass player.

One day in 1987 the Bullfiddler was substitute teaching at Johnston High School in East Austin when the Austin Symphony put on a gig for the students. After the show Dr. Neubert talked with Bullfiddler and asked Bullfiddler if he still had a receipt for his bullfiddle. While studying with Dr. Neubert the Bullfiddler bought his first bullfiddle from an instrument dealer out of Houston who was referred to Bullfiddler by Dr. Neubert. The dealer and Bullfiddler made arrangements one night to meet at a motel in South Austin where the instrument dealer sold Bullfiddler a bullfiddle in mint condition with shiny brass tuning keys, good action on the neck and a suburb finish on the wood. Now Bullfiddler had two bullfiddles, the one he just bought and the old Kay student bass he had checked out for two semesters from UT's music room. With Dr. Neubert's permission Bullfiddler traded in that good lookin' great soundin' bullfiddle for the old plywood Kay with the warped fingerboard. The trade was made for foolish sentimental reasons. At Johnston High Dr. Neubert asked Bullfiddler if he still had the receipt for that trade.

"That was over two years ago. I never got a receipt,' the Bullfiddler told him.

"Well, we are missing a double bass from our inventory," Dr. Neubert said.

"I still have the UT serial number on this thing', the Bullfiddler said and anxiously showed Dr. Neubert the UT serial number concealed under a bumper sticker advertising a south Austin juke joint. The Bullfiddler was getting more nervous as he walked Dr. Neubert to his car.

"The kid that ran the music room was your TA", Bullfiddler said. "I never thought to ask for a receipt."

"I'm pokin' yer eyes," Dr Neubert said and Bullfiddler breathed a sigh of relief.

Bullfiddlers first band job as Bullfiddler after being fired from Debbie Norrad and Pure Country was as a part of a duet with Tony Brassatt. The duo was billed as The Raindogs, and Tony later went on the help form an Austin jazz group 'The 'Jazz Pharaohs'. Tony and the Bullfiddler met at an open mic at the Austin Outhouse and this time the two had band photos taken and rehearsed diligently. Together Tony and Bullfiddler played at The Outhouse, Ravens Garage on 6th street, and various open mics around Austin. Often they played somewhere every night of the week but it was when the Raindogs literally played 'on the street' down on '6th Street' that things got hairy.

The Raindogs found a spot across the street from Ravens Garage on 6th street right off the busy crowded sidewalk. The duo set up an open guitar case and played for tips sometimes making as much as $40 each a night. They played on that outdoor spot every Friday and Saturday night for six months. While playing for the sidewalk crowd one crowded weekend night a man was standing in front of Bullfiddler intensely watching him play his bullfiddle. In the middle of a song the stranger maliciously grabbed Bullfiddlers nipples with both hands, squeezed them hard and quickly disappeared into the crowd. The Raindogs had witnessed fights and a stabbing while doing their 'internship' on 6th street, but they closed up shop and never went back to the streets after that incident preferring to play small dates in cafes and opening for other bands. When Tony Brassatt left the Raindogs to form 'The Jazz Pharaohs' Tony immediately became very popular jazz clubs in Austin.

Chapter 11

OPEN MICS

The Bullfiddler began to back other people up at open mics and by the mid-80's there were many open mics in Austin. Karaoke had not caught on yet and aspiring musicians would get on the open mic circuit sometimes playing as many as 12 different stages a week. Musicians would try out their new songs and see what did and did not work with the audiences. Amateur singer songwriters met fellow musicians and became accustomed to performing in front of various diverse crowds. Teri Hendrix is as fine an example of someone who used the Austin open mic scene to hone her stage skills and her music. Teri lived in San Marcos and in the mid-to late 1980's she performed every night of the week and often twice a night on different Austin stages while commuting from San Marcos, 23 miles south of Austin. Always sober and refreshingly friendly she eventually teamed up with Loyd Maines, signed recording contracts and began playing her snappy witty original music all over the world including tapings for Austin City Limits and on Nashville recording sessions. Teri has since recorded some excellent CDs and has earned the love and respect of thousands of music lovers.

The Bullfiddler continued his practice of picking up paying dates wherever possible. Austin has some fine music schools at The University of Texas, St. Edwards and Concordia Lutheran Universities and the Austin Community College and yet Bullfiddler remained an illiterate musician, unable to read quickly a standard music chart. Consequently he hooked up with other amateur musicians while professional touring musicians like those in Asleep at The Wheel, Joe King Carrasco and Beto y los Fairlanes advertised on music school bulletin boards around Austin for musicians who could read arrangements. The Bullfiddler preferred typed lyric sheets with the notes in capital letters atop the word they are to be played. Often these 'charts' substituted numbers for notes. When a chart is set up with numbers a musician can play the song any key the bandleader requires. Bullfiddler got into the habit of memorizing songs when working with a band.

At the open mics like the Threadgill's Sittin' Singin' Supper Sessions the musicians might work up a number in the bar back office or in the parking lot or backyard. These are referred to as 'head' charts since no music or music stands were ever used. It wasn't until Bullfiddler began playing music at church in 2003 that he started using a music stand during performances, although he would rarely look at the music charts. For some the music stand can be a shield to hide behind. Bullfiddler was later amazed at a Rolling Stones concert in San Antonio in 2001 to see Mick Jagger and the band with a teleprompter even though the Stones had been singing most of their songs since the sixties and seventies.

Richard Patureau played an open mic at The Austin Outhouse one night and Bullfiddler was there with his Kay bullfiddle. Together Bullfiddler and Richard rehearsed three songs in the Outhouse back yard and then performed them to an appreciative audience. Richard hired Bullfiddler that night and asked Bullfiddler to play his electric Fender bass on his project, a collection of fifty two original and three cover songs, all with a Louisiana cajun feel. For some reason Richard, like Debbie Norrad preferred a standard electric bass. Richard had previously played bass for the Supernatural Family Band at the Shorthorn Lounge two years earlier and graciously let Bullfiddler once sit in on his bass for two songs. He remembered his encounter with the Bulllfiddler at The Shorthorn Lounge an independent biker bar just a few steps south of The Stallion Restaurant where Bullfiddler was employed as a prep cook.

As a trio, Richard, John Logan and Bullfiddler hosted an open mic at a bar called the Little Wheel on Highway 290 near Johnson city. Richard Patureau and The Bayou Bandits developed an efficient system. Richard would come over to Bullfiddlers apartment on Monday with three charts and they would run through the songs once. Richard would leave Bullfiddler a tape and Bullfiddler would practice the three songs during the week. The Bandits would then perform the songs at the Little Wheel on Sunday afternoons while hosting an open mic. The open mic often included such fine Texas musicians such as the Wimberley Volunteer Fireants, Emily Kaitz and the Lounge Lizards. The Bandits had band photos taken of the three poking their heads out of Bullfiddlers 1978 cherry red Cadillac deVille in the bar parking lot. Gas at the time was $1.35 or so a gallon.

The Bandits system went on for a year and the band eventually ended up in a recording studio in Hyde Park in central Austin. Simultaneously the band took Richards music 'on the road', playing La Grange, Elgin, Bastrop, Victoria, and various bars up and down east highway 71. The Bandits played their fifty-two originals and two or three covers and were never rebooked or asked back. The musical rejections plus the fact that Richard's wife, his pretty college sweetheart was divorcing him and taking the kids was making music difficult for Richard to deal with.

Chapter 12

FIRED!

During one rehearsal in the garage of Richards two-story north Austin home Bullfiddler began talking about the 'underground railroad' he participated in El Paso where he helped soldiers going through 'Basic' or 'Advanced Infantry Training' escape Vietnam by getting a six-month Mexican visa and taking a train to Guadalajara, Mexico from Juarez. The Bullfiddler told of how he used his dad's old notary public seal to fabricate documents so the soldiers could obtain Mexican entry visas. Bullfiddler related how he often hid awol soldiers in his apartment until they were ready to leave the country. Once the soldiers were gone for thirty days they were classified as deserters. Richard had a sound man who occasionally played harmonica on some of the songs while simultaneously running the sound board during band gigs and rehearsals. It turned out the guy was still in the military with eighteen months left until retirement. He sternly informed Bullfiddler that he had done three tours of 'Nam and had eight months to go before his retirement from the Army. That weekend after the Bandits finished their three song set at the Little Wheel, Richard asked Bullfiddler if he wanted a drink at the bar. Bullfiddler knew something was up.

"Whadda ya have, Bullfiddler?" Richard asked.

"Anything?" Bullfiddler asked.

"Whatever you want," Richard said.

The Bullfiddler knew something was up and ordered a Wild Turkey double. Richard proceeded to politely tell Bullfiddler that he felt Bullfiddler didn't "have the feel" for the music, this was Bullfiddlers last gig with the Bandits and there were no hard feeling's. Bullfiddler knew his firing was due to the attitude of the pissed off veteran soundman who by obviously despised Bullfiddler with a passion. After that experience the Bullfiddler was very careful about discussing politics in a musical setting.

Bullfiddler had his first Austin studio recording experience on that Bandit project and he did get credit on the album that flopped and almost bankrupted Richard. Richard later quit the music business after trying to avoid his divorce, sold his amps and other musical gear and went back to selling insurance. Bullfiddler felt this was a shame because Richard Patureau is a good songwriter. Two songs Bullfiddler worked on in the studio were 'Never Say Goodbye' and 'The Shorthorn Bar'. Bullfiddler went back to open mics and more pickup gigs.

The Austin Outhouse was a magnet for songwriters and Bullfiddler went through a period in the mid 1980's where he wrote 21 songs. Luckily Bullfiddler had an upstairs neighbor, Billy Benton who agreed to arrange his songs songs. Bullfiddler would give Billy a cassette with a new single song (guitar and vocals) along with typed lyric sheet with the basic chords and within three or four days Billy would bring back an arrangement written in both the treble and bass clef, charging Bullfiddler ten dollars per arrangement.

In 1988 Bullfiddler self-published those songs 'Playin' Music' via St. Edwards University. He was fortunate to sell ten or eleven copies of the book but nobody picked up any of the songs to record. The songs were, a good friend of the Bullfiddler said: "fluff compared to the music of such deep thinkers as Blaze Foley, Towns Van Zandt and Willie Nelson. One song, 'Sweet Outhouse' was written about a woman who got out of prison after two and a half years and rejoiced in returning th her old haunt. At the same time 'Playin' Music' came out Bullfiddler also wrote a manual 'Piano Tuning for Tone Deaf Dummies'. That work was never published and received no interest but the exercise did further Bullfiddlers interest in piano.

Bullfiddlers next band job was with rockabilly Tony Pulgese who had the stage name Tony Masaratti. Tony is a rockabilly connesouir, buying and selling vintage records at Austin record conventions. His rockabilly band was called 'Tony and The Tigers'. Tony, an avid old time rockabilly fan would look for the 'odd' cuts on old '50's rockabilly albums and have the Tigers learn and perform those obscure songs with Tony playing his expensive red Gretch guitar. His Gretch guitar had an odd characteristic in that if one string broke the rest of the strings on the guitar go way out of tune. Tony for years had only that Gretch and the band often had to take a break whenever Tony broke a string.

When the Bullfiddler joined The Tigers Tony was playing with lead guitarist James Merideth. After joining the Tigers the trio rehearsed in the living room of James' small apartment four times a week for two weeks before they began playing in public. Tony did never like to play with a drummer and insisted Bullfiddler 'slap' his bullfiddle furiously to the feverish rock and roll beats. Bullfiddler played two roles in the Tigers, bassist and percussionist.

It was during Bullfiddlers tenure with Tony and the Tigers that he began to occasionally experience a major cramp in his left forearm during gigs. When this happened, a painful knot the size of a golf ball popped up on Bullfiddlers left forearm and his fingers grew temporarily stiff and unmovable making it very difficult to play the acoustic bass. The cramp always quickly went away and its cause could have been the loud volume and poor amplification that, Bullfiddler believed caused the cramp. Tony and the Tigers was a very loud band and and Bullfiddler played the bass hard to be heard over screaming James Merideth guitar leads. Maybe if Bullfiddler had a decent amp that played 'loud' clearly, or the Tigers played quieter the cramps never would have happened. The forearm cramp appeared on rare unexpected occasions when Bullfiddler played with Tony and The Tigers, always in the middle of a rollicking song, and only once during a gig. The cramp would subside as quickly as it arose and fortionately did not become a real concern.

Chapter 13

CURLEY

On one off Friday night in 1987 Bullfiddler went to the Victory Bar and Grill on East 11th Street in Austin to support a local blues project and eat a plate of delicious mesquite cooked barbecue. There he met and sat in with Curley a talented drummer who would become a friend of Bullfiddler's for life. Curley is not only a drummer he also has the vocal range of Roy Orbison and was not afraid of anyone or trying anything. Curley was rough and liked to play 'quick draw' but only once did he take someone down physically while hanging out with Bullfiddler at Thundercloud Subs on Riverside Drive and that was because a drunk hit him first. Curley took the drunk to the concrete floor quickly without harming him. When not playing music Curley had been a bouncer at The Austex Lounge, the Armadillo, Beverlies and other Austin venues. He was in demand as a bouncer because he was not a bully and believed in fair play.

Curley did time for almost killing his step father in defense of his abused mother. On his return to Austin after doing his state time became involved in the music world and quickly became locally famous and well-loved by people and fellow musicians all over Austin. Curley and Bullfiddler formed a rhythm section with Curley on snare and Bullfiddler on his bullfiddle. He could play drums as good as Gene Kruppa due in part to training Curley received from his natural father, a Los Angeles studio musician who played on studio recordings with Johnny Rivers, the Ventures and other Californians.

Together the two played interesting gigs at places like the Banditos hangout, Beverlies with hot motorcycle oil smells drifting over the stage, the Shorthorn Lounge on North Lamar or the Hole in the Wall. The Austin Chronicle used Curley's picture for months on the Chronicles entire back cover page advertising an Austin bar. When and wherever Curley and the Bullfiddler went, the band playing and the crowd would call Curley up on stage where he would either play drums, sing or play harmonica. Curley could play and sound great on harmonica with or without an actual harmonica. A natural entertainer he would never play music with Bullfiddler at a paying gig if Bullfiddler had been drinking. Together Curley and Bullfiddler hosted an open mic at Stubb's BBQ, C.B. Stubbafield's restaurant on the North Central I-35 access road next to the railroad tracks. Stubbs was very good to musicians; he payed them and gave performers a free dinner and limited amounts of Lone Star beer.

On one special occasion Curley and Bullfiddler played a benefit for Blaze Foley's funeral expenses at Charlies Attic on Airport Blvd. in East Austin. The bar sat atop a hamburger restaurant and smelled of hamburger meat and onions. The two carried drums and amps upstairs and found themselves gigging with Mike Ochs on lead guitar, Banda on background vocals featuring Cody Heubock on rhythm guitar and lead vocals. There was a large tape machine sitting in front of the stage with an engineer operating it but nobody, not even Cody's wife seems to know where that tape ended up. It might have been published. Cody Heubock was a good friend of Blaze Foley and also a regular performer at the Austin Outhouse. He had two 45 rpm records he recorded in the mid-70's on the Outhouse jukebox. In 1997 Cody with the help of long-time friend John Casner released his only self titled CD. His CD release parties were in Spicewood Springs at Poodies on Highway 71 and at Giddy-Ups in Manchaca. Cody's wife gave Cody a stone bust of his head she had carved in secret. The bust is remarkable and looks just like Cody.

Shortly after Cody's album release parties Bullfiddler while drinking with a new friend at the third and last Soap Creek Saloon at the intersection of Academy and Congress decided to drive to El Paso for the weekend. El Paso is halfway between Austin and San Diego California and by the time Bullfiddler and his friend sobered up they were almost to El Paso. After fourteen sweaty hours on the road they reached El Paso entering the city on the same freeway that can be seen in Steve McQueen's movie 'The Getaway'. Once there Bullfiddler could find none of his friends. They had all either left town or died off. One old girlfriend was married with children. The two did meet with Richard Lasini who was now finding musical fulfillment playing music for his church. They ate lunch at the Oasis Cafe some three blocks north of the Copacabana which morphed into a 'Ropa Usada' store. The lunch went quickly and Richard insisted the two walk Richard to his car so he could show off his new Cadillac convertible parked out in front of the Oasis. Bullfiddlers parents were gone and his siblings were scattered around the Midwest so within a few hours the two were itching to get back to Austin and their jobs, music and their many friends.

Back in Austin Bullfiddler via a real estate agent in Bastrop bought some forested land in the sweet smelling blue-green pine covered hills on the outskirts of Bastrop. Bullfiddler desperately wanted to have something to show for his efforts in Austin so he prorated the down payment for the land and then found himself obligated to the land payments or risk losing both land and equity. As his equity increased with each monthly payment he also had to pay rent in Austin which in 1986 was two hundred fifty dollars a month plus electricity. Bullfiddler could not afford both rent and land payments so he moved into a Volkswagen van until two years later when he traded the land for another parcel in the heavily wooded Bastrop Pines off Highway 21. The trade gave him the land outright and all he had to do was pay minimal property taxes. Now Bullfiddler was a landowner and could again afford to rent an apartment, shower regularly and enjoy his paid utilities. Television was still free and for the first time in his adult life Bullfiddler bought a television and began to watch it, thinking he had earned the right to self indulge in mindless entertainment. Proudly he now had a financial stake in Austin.

The Bastrop land was eventually sold to a Mexican-American family. A few months after the sale was complete the United States Army notified Bullfiddler that there might be unexploded ordinance on the property and that they were going to come out and search the property for any lost ordinance. Bullfiddler could imagine the Chicano families surprise when the United States Army knocked on their door and paid the unsuspecting family and their property a thorough visit. Bullfiddler failed to notify the family of the impending land search having thrown away any paperwork related to the land or its sale. All this time Bullfiddler was gigging in and around Austin and enjoying the musician's life to the max.

Chapter 14

MUSIC THERAPY

While playing with Tony and The Tigers Bullfiddler heard that the Austin State Hospital paid bands $40.00 to entertain the 'consumers' as the patients were called at that time. The gigs were for only one hour. As a three-piece rockabilly group the Tigers often played the hour-long gigs at the Austin State Hospital. The Tigers played their first gig at the Austin State Hospital, (ASH), on a week day afternoon and after admitting themselves through the unmanned Guadalupe Street gate and finding a parking spot, the Tigers were led to a small theater. ASH provided the PA, Tony and James lined out into the small house PA and Bullfiddler went through an Ampeg amp. The consumers were led in and The Tigers rockabillied causing consumers in the audience to get up and dance. The audience reaction was overwhelming and the gig was Bullfiddler's first introduction to music therapy.

Both the staff and the consumers at ASH liked The Tigers and the band ended up playing at ASH once every three months for the next two years, occasionally performing for ASH's big Valentine's dance held annually in the huge institutional gymnasium. They never did get used to the sweaty earthy smells of the auditorium. The Tigers played at ASH one afternoon and the Austin Chronicle got wind of what The Tigers were doing and arranged to take a band photo of the Tigers standing beside the ASH sign on Guadalupe Street. At that fortunate moment in time John X Reed substituted for James Merideth on both the photo shoot and on his always stunning lead guitar while playing a vintage Fender Telecaster.

The Bullfiddler kept up his contact with ASH and later developed an association with the Austin State School who unlike the State Hospital, didn't pay any money; all State School gigs were volunteer gigs only. The State School has a pseudo 'night club' called Neos on the grounds that looked like a bar but only served cokes to the MR consumers that attended the gigs. There were occasions when Musician's Union musicians played at Neo's. The union musicians would fill out forms, have the State School honcho sign them and send them to the Musicians Performance Trust Fund. In a few months the Fund would a send the musician scale for the gig that they had all but forgotten.

It was with Tony and The Tigers that Bullfiddler did more studio work and had his first television appearance and videos. In the Austin Access studio James Merideth, Tony and Bullfiddler recorded 'Money Honey' 'Who You Been Lovin'' and 'Milk Cow Blues' among others. James also called Bullfiddler into the studio later that week to record a song for a friend of James', Theresa Locke. The three recorded 'Angel Baby' and the song was later used by Theresa as a demo and was not widely distributed. These recordings were done at AWOL Studios and James later recorded two more songs at AWOL with Bullfiddler for his personal demo. They recorded 'Jimmies Kitchen' and 'Cowboy Blues' under the band name Blues Buckaroos.

In 1987 Bullfiddler had a one-shot opportunity to record live at The Continental Club with Jimmy R. Harrell. Without prior rehearsal Harrell and Bullfiddler and two other fine musicians recorded among other songs 'Gotta Love Someone' and 'Trouble in Mind'. During that session one of the musicians came up with an amplified accordion and played it on one song leaving Bullfiddlers' hair on the nape of his neck tingling. Jimmy Harrell gave Bullfiddler a copy of two of the recorded songs and that was the last time they played together.

Austin for years had a city sponsored music channel, Channel 15. Local bands would either be taped at a gig or come into the studio in east Austin and tape a set for an up coming show. The Tigers arrived at the eastside studio, set up their gear and went outside. After taping a roaring rockabilly session all three of the Tigers were briefly interviewed and the show was later and often broadcast on Austin access television. When viewing this amateur video is irritating to watch close-ups of Tony singing because the microphone kept bouncing back and fourth almost smacking Tony in the mouth. Later on rare occasions people came up to band members and said they saw them on television and their young egos swelled with pride; the Tigers were on Austin Television.

Tony booked a gig at the Deep Eddy Cabaret in Clarksville on the west-central side of Austin. The Cabaret is a small bar with no stage so The Tigers set up on the floor next to the juke box. There was so little room that the young hot shot lead guitarist (one of many who substituted for James Merideth or John X Reed) placed his Fender Reverb amp on top of Bullfiddlers bass amp. The Tigers were very loud that night and that lead guitar was right in Bullfiddlers ears at head level. The Deep Eddy Cabaret gig was the loudest stage volume gig Bullfiddler ever played.

On another occasion Tony and the Tigers played a Friday night date in a bar in deserted Deep Ellum in Dallas. All three of The Tigers had worked all week at their day jobs and after the gig was over the band loaded up the gear in Tony's van and headed back to Austin, all three exhausted. James Merideth was asleep in the front passenger seat, Bullfiddler was in the back seat coughing from a quick onset of flu and Tony was driving fast down I-35 toward Austin. Bullfiddler suddenly felt rough bumping, looked out the front window and noticed the van heading off the road toward a ditch at 60 miles per hour. Bullfiddler yelled and Tony awoke in time to right the van and get back on on the road. He refused to let Bullfiddler drive so Bullfiddler talked constantly to Tony until they finished the trip to Austin, getting home at 3:30 am.

In 1989 Bullfiddler moved on to play regularly with a tame eclectic folk-jazz-rock band called BNL Revue but still occasionally played with Tony and the Tigers on non-BNL Revue nights. Eventually Tony and the Tigers just tired of each other and parted on friendly terms. After years spent playing three-chord songs the music can get dull unless one is a real rockabilly aficionado. The folk-jazz coming from BNL Revue was all rockabilly was not. The lyrics and multi-faceted music had depth and made rockabilly seem like small potatoes in comparison to BNL Revue's varied style. At the time Bullfiddler was still renting an efficiency apartment for two-hundred twenty-five dollars plus electricity and had no problems paying any of his bills. Bullfiddler was driving himself to gigs in a 1979 six cylinder Ford truck with a half camper shell on the back. By now he always had to have a vehicle that could accommodate a bullfiddle, an amplifier and could be locked up. Unlike other musicians Bullfiddler was never ripped off, but he played his share of benefits for musicians who were victims of theft. BNL Revue played a benefit up stairs at Katz' for the blind band Blue Mist. The band's manager left all their gear in their van overnight after a gig and the van with guitars, amps, microphones and drums was stolen later that early morning. Band members noticed the theft when they went outside to unload their gear the next morning. Blue Mist was well loved by many all over Austin and there were numerous benefits all over town on their behalf. Their gear was never recovered but the band with the help of the Austin music community never missed any of their scheduled gigs.

Chapter 15

RECORDING IN AUSTIN

In 1989 Bullfiddler met Michael Ochs a Pennsylvania transplant at an open mic at Austin's Thundercloud Subs on Riverside Drive. Mike was playing guitar in BNL Revue and the band needed a bass player. Mike and Bullfiddler hit it off right away and Mike later introduced Bullfiddler to the rest of the band: Eve Kunianski, an engineer working with the Federal Government played alto sax and flute, Marcella Elmer Garcia a talented bilingual vocalist, Georgina, the blind tenor sax player and Robert Sarcinella, a drummer with an engineering degree from Texas Tech who also worked for the State of Texas Highway Department. Mike and Bullfiddler rehearsed intensely at Mikes South Austin apartment. This was convenient for Bullfiddler because at the time he was teaching at St. Edwards University part-time and the school was close to Mike's apartment. It wasn't very long before Bullfiddler was playing his bullfiddle at some of Austin's interesting live music cafes, Scholtz Beer Garden, The Green Mesquite, The Dam Cafe out at lake Mansfield and Artz Ribhouse, to name a few. It was a gig at the Dam Cafe that caused Bullfiddler to make a resolution he would keep for life.

    The no-name-band played on the outdoor stage surrounded by Harley Davidson motorcycles. Bullfiddler had played there twice before and on this particular night a large full orange harvest moon slowly arose casting light on the party and the outdoor stage. As usual there were no fights, lots of dancing, laughter and loud motorcycles. The bikers treated the band well whenever they played there. After the show the no-name-band packed up and headed out to an all night cafe on the I-35 access road called appropriately, The Stars Inn for dinner, coffee and gain energy to unload their gear. While driving down the dark sparsely populated South Congress avenue after the harvest moon gig, Bullfiddler had to hit the breaks to keep from hitting a body lying in the road. Luckily the stowed gear did not slide forward and crush Bullfiddler or

Curley as he sat rigid in the passenger seat. Bullfiddler pulled the loaded car off Congress and shone the headlights on the body of a woman. They noticed a few yards down the road that there was a motorcycle and two more people were lying on the road.

The accident involved a couple riding the Harley home when the motorcycle hit a woman pedestrian as she crossed Congress. The pedestrian died that night, the biker had a broken left arm and his girl friend spent two weeks at St. David's Hospital. The no-name-band was the last band that dead woman partied with that night. After the accident at The Dam Cafe during a full moon two years later while playing with BNL Revue, Bullfiddler decided that he would never again play at a biker bar during a full moon.

While playing with BNL Revue one night at the Dam Cafe Bullfiddler met the father of one of Bullfiddler's former students. Jimmy Carl Black was the drummer for Frank Zappas Mothers of Invention while Bullfiddler was teaching English to Jimmy's daughter in Anthony, New Mexico. Unlike Jimmy, his daughter was always conservatively dressed, a good student and very quiet. Bullfiddler remembered a friendly conference with Jimmy one night in a bar in Anthony New Mexico. At that time Jimmy and his family lived in the country between El Paso, Texas and Las Cruces, New Mexico while Jimmy was off on his adventures with Frank Zappa. Anthony is a small desert town half in Texas and half in New Mexico and Bullfiddler held two concurrent jobs with the New Mexican school district; he taught English and was the publicity director for the Anthony New Mexico Independent School District.

The parent-teacher conference with Jimmy Carl was one of Bullfiddlers highlights that school year. They discussed Jimmy's part in Zappas and the Mothers movie 200 Motels and Bullfiddler praised Jimmies daughter, pointing out that she was a good well-behaved student. Jimmy later went on to form his own group, The Grandmothers touring extensively all over Europe. Bullfiddler did not recognize Jimmy Carl until Jimmy sat at the drum kit and played on a couple of BNL Revue songs. Jimmy's daughter, he later told Bullfiddler graduated from high school and took a job with El Paso National Bank. She was Jimmy's exact opposite; she was quiet and ultra-conservative. Jimmy signed Bullfiddler's bullfiddle with the inscription "To my daughters teacher, thanks". The Bullfiddler had begun letting musicians sign his bullfiddle and every time Bullfiddler looked at a signature on his bullfiddle he thought back to a particular gig. The Bullfiddler picked up that idea from reading 'The Illustrated Man'.

One night during Bullfiddler's tenure with BNL Revue he spent an off night at the Austin Outhouse where Tom Shaka played for the bartender, Bullfiddler and one other customer. Tom sat in a chair on the wooden stage and stomped his steel reinforced boots on the stage floor to create a strong rhythm for his exciting invigorating music. Tom Shaka, a very solid entertainer is an American ex-patriot who lives and gigs in Germany. At the time he played the Outhouse he was visiting Austin while touring the States, returning to Germany three weeks later. The Bullfiddler talked with Tom at the Outhouse during his break and later that week met him at Whole Foods where Tom invited Bullfiddler to play bass with him at his upcoming gig at the Hole in the Wall bar. Bullfiddler turned him down because he had another gig that night. A few months later, while looking at Beatles books in the music section of the Austin Public Library Bullfiddler opened a book on the Beatles and on the first page was a photo of Tony Sheridan and Tom Shaka, and on the following page was a photo of Tom Shaka sitting on a stool playing his guitar. Tom and Tony Sheridan and The Beatles hung out together and learned the German phrase 'mach sho" while working in tough German bars. Had Bullfiddler known of Tom's prior association with the Beatles he would have played that gig for free, offered to buy Tom dinner and would have gladly listened to him talk about the 'old days' for hours. This incident is an example of the kind of musical stuff that happens all the time in Austin.

In 1991 BNL Revue released a cassette 'BNL Revue Live'. The compilation received good reviews in the press for both the writing and the musicianship. All the songs were original and Bullfiddler was the only one who did not have a song on that cassette. He had been asked if he had anything to contribute but declined, much to his later regret. Before the cassette was released BNL Revue helped Eve build a recording studio in her home. Eve and the bands drummer, Bob Sarcenilla are professional engineers and they and the rest of the band built that studio from her specifications. This included carpentry, installing the recording machines in an isolated control booth, acoustic insulation, everything a professional studio would need to make good recordings. Building that studio was an education for everyone on the project culminating with the studio's first recording with BNL Revue's 'Live' project. Actually they recorded the music one track at a time in Eve's new studio she now called ELK Audio. The BNL Revue Live cassette was later released as a CD in 1997.

Bullfiddler was disappointed with the album cover because it was a pen and ink drawing of the band and Bullfiddler appeared very bald while standing with his bullfiddle. With feelings of musical accomplishment Bullfiddler gave out those tapes and later the CD's annually for various Christmases and birthdays. The cassette included Eve Kuniansky on flute, mandolin, vocals and sax, Marcie Lane on vocals and percussion, Bullfiddler on acoustic and electric bass, Michael Ochs on guitar, vocals and harmonica and Robert 'Sarc—inella on drums with Michael Shemp is listed as knobster. On that project Michael Ochs wrote 'Celia', 'Gambling Blues', 'Morning Blues' and 'Runaway and Dance'. Eve wrote 'Encounters', 'Head over Heels' and 'Why' and Robert Sarcinella wrote and sang 'Granger Bay'.

One night at Ruby's Barbecue House next door to Antones on Guadalupe Street BNL Revue was playing outdoors in the beer garden. On this warm summer evening Bullfiddler was playing his bullfiddle while standing in the rear to on the drummers right. Bullfiddler looked up during the band's rendition of 'Daddy Longlegs', to notice that the lead singer, Marcella Garcia did not have her shirt on. There were no children in the audience and BNL Revue finished that song with Marcie giving the crowd a little more than her beautiful voice. The drummer and Bullfiddler were able to laugh and keep time without losing a beat.

On occasion the band at Antones next door to Ruby's BBQ would start up as BNL Revue was finishing their last set. The Bullfiddler could hear the blues band playing loud and would play bass along with the blues for a few bars. Clifford Antone, everyone knew, loved the blues and Bullfiddler hoped to play at Antone's someday. His date with Antone's never happened. In 1992 Bullfiddler quit BNL Revue and let Georgina the band's blind tenor sax player play bass. Georgina always said she would rather play bass than sax but for the money Georgina is one of the best 'hard' rock and roll horn players one could ever play music with. The Bullfiddler was working now with Austin-Travis County Mental Health and Mental Retardation, putting in up to 70 hours a week.

In 1989, prior to his employment with ATCMHMR, Bullfiddler had three part-time jobs working simultaneously at St. Edwards University, The Austin Independent School District as a substitute teacher, and the Texas School for The Blind as a substitute teacher in the life skills department. Bullfiddler traded the three jobs in to work full-time with ATCMHMR. While teaching at St Edward's University Bullfiddler had the opportunity to play a song with Little Joe Hernandez of Little Joe y La Familia. Little Joe was the commencement speaker that year. Bullfiddler had a student that wanted to perform a song for the commencement activities. The student and Bullfiddler worked up Spanish language song the student wanted to perform. The two rehearsed the song for two weeks, the student teaching Bullfiddler some Spanish and Bullfiddler contributed to the songs arrangement. At the commencement banquet the two performed the song with the student singing lead vocals and playing guitar. After the two finished the song, the student asked Little Joe if he would sing a song with the duo. This caught Bullfiddler off guard as Little Joe Hernandez joined the musicians for a well-done corrida.

Another facet of the Austin music scene is the music therapy programs going on all over Travis County. Bullfiddler had been working for ATCMHMR for more than a few months when he teemed up musically with Jack Knox, a psychologist and Ruben Maldonado a caseworker. Their first gig was at Rosedale Elementary School. The as yet unnamed band did not rehearse but ended up playing old Country and rock and roll 'covers' for numerous functions for Travis County's mentally retarded population. The trio had no original songs and after a year the band agreed to let themselves be billed as Los Downbeats, the altered name of Bullfiddlers first band in El Paso. Consequently, Los Downbeats became well known with the huge mentally retarded community in Austin. Performing for ATCMHMR client activities led to gigging occasionally for outside functions.

Los Downbeats played at dances for the Austin mental health population at places like McBeth Recreation, Hyde Park Methodist Church, Hancock Recreation Center, Marbridge Ranch just outside Manchaca, Texas and the ATCMHMR campouts at the agency's lakeside campsite outside of Leander, Texas. Both Lupe Maldonado and Jack Knox could have had music careers because they are were outstanding musicians great story tellers, sang well and had a lot of confidence and personality. ATCMHMR held an annual Thanksgiving dinner at Austins Hyde Park Methodist Church and Bullfiddlers Los Downbeats played for there often for the church dances. During the Thanksgiving dinner of 1993 someone introduced Bullfiddler to Don Walser, a large man with a large voice who volunteered to sing at the Thanksgiving church dance for free.

Don Walser was developing a well-earned following but when he met Bullfiddler, the Bullfiddler did not know Don or of his budding reputation. The Bullfiddler asked Don if he could sit in with Don on some of his songs when Don played the show. Don, a very generous man gave Bullfiddler the OK. Together they set up the PA on the stage and Don asked Bullfiddler to play at the beginning of his set. The two played Don's entire show and it was later that evening that Bullfiddler met 'Too Slim', Don's regular old friend bass player. Don and Too Slim let Bullfiddler play the show using 'Too Slim's very old Fender Precision bass. Later when the agency asked Bullfiddler to book gigs for the agency's annual fundraiser at Auditorium Shores, Don Walser was first on Bullfiddlers list to call, and the first in a long line of prominent performers to perform for the annual fundraiser.

During this period Bullfiddler married for a second time and together with his bride they raised her son, a quiet, intelligent boy who could sit on a front porch and talk for hours without feeling he had to run off and do things. Bullfiddler was introduced to his second-x-to-be by a friend of BNL Revue and the wedding was held at Barton Springs with an informal acoustic jam after the ceremony. Mike Ochs played his banjo and guitar, Eve was on flute, Georgina was on tenor sax and Bullfiddler played his bullfiddle. They drew a crowd and made a few new friends.

Bullfiddler rehearsed his Los Downbeats in the living room of their house on Franklin Avenue a short distance from Wallar Creek. When Los Downbeats picked up a gig featuring music from the 20's and 30's, Stan 'Pops' played clarinet with long haired professional Boomer Norman on guitar. The clarinet player had an influence on Bullfiddlers young stepson and the boy signed up for the school band at Riley Elementary School with clarinet as his instrument. However, he did not like the school band and could not play the clarinet. The boy was bringing home D's in band on his report card and told Bullfiddler he just did not 'feel it'. One afternoon Bullfiddler asked the boy to set up his clarinet so he could see what the boy did know. After the boy unpacked and assembled the clarinet and set the reed the boy began to run through warm-up exercises.

Bullfiddler stopped the boy, found the key he was warming up in and asked him to play the warm-up when Bullfiddler gave the boy the signal. Bullfiddler then began strumming guitar chords and nodded at the boy who began playing his warm-up exercises. Together they were in the same key and in tune and Bullfiddler will never forget how the boys eyes grew large with amazement as he free associated in the jam with Bullfiddler.

The boy made a 'D' in band, returned the clarinet to the school and after high school began playing electric bass which he later played with a couple of young bands in Austin. Bullfiddler and his second wife divorced after seven years with no animosity. He will never forget the day she came home and said she was leaving, that she had found "a 19 year-old long distance bicycle rider with buns of steel". Bullfiddler thought it interesting that while they were dating she came to all his performances but after the wedding she devoted herself to school and rarely accompanied Bullfiddler to any of his shows. By this time Bullfiddlers new family was renting a two bedroom house for three hundred dollars a month plus bills. The house was right under the flight path to the old Mueller Airport and Bullfiddler remembers how eerie the environment became the day the airplanes stopped flying overhead when air traffic was switched to Bergstrom. As with trains, Bullfiddler could tolerate the noise and when the neighborhood quieted down, property values began to rise and development began to happen. For eight years Bullfiddlers landlord never raised the rent while neighbors began tearing down their old homes, replacing them with two story mini-mansions.

Chapter 16

BOOKING GIGS

Lupe Maldanado was a case working co-worker of Bullfiddlers who came to Austin from the Harlingen-McAllen area. He could sing just as good as Freddie Fender and rocked in both English and Spanish, teaching Bullfiddler 'The Chicken Song'. One day Lupe came into Bullfiddlers office and told him the agency (ATCMHMR) needed someone to book the annual fundraiser 'The Rib Ticklin' Affair', an outdoor barbecue cook-off held at Auditorium Shores annually in early September. This event occurred during Austin's dog days of summer in mid-September with no breeze and 100 degree plus heat. There was no extra pay for booking these Auditorium Shores concerts and coordinating the shows but Bullfiddler jumped for the chance to get involved and he ended up booking some of Austin's most well-known acts over a six-year period. One of Stevie Ray Vaughn's backup band members had a business called 'Ample Sound' who provided public address systems for concerts. The company provided not only a good PA but also sober smart and fast technicians who were very professional. Bullfiddler scheduled 20 minute time limits on the break down and set up between acts and the entertainment part of the fundraiser ran smoothly year after year without a hitch.

One of the more interesting shows Bullfiddler booked during his stint as entertainment coordinator for ATCMHMR was the Fifth Annual Rib Ticklin' Affair on September 17th, 1994. El Kabong opened the show at 11:30 am. El Kabong was a hard driving rock and roll band performing music from the '60's and '70's as well as some originals. Besides performing for the Rib Ticklin' events El Kabong regularly played at Patos Tacos, Las Brisas on Lake Travis and private parties. Bob Hernandez played guitar, Rudy Sanchez played bass and Coby Ramirez played drums. All three sang and had great harmonies.

The next act was Joseph Vincelli a saxophone player. Bullfiddler met him through a press kit submission; at that time Vincelli was releasing his newest CD 'The Time Has Come'. Vincelli had opened for Marcia Ball, played for the Dallas Cowboys and held down regular horn playing gigs at Antone's Joseph had an interesting history; he recorded with Bobby Goldsboro, Buddy Miles, Bob Hope, Rosanne Arnold and Bert Reynolds.

On the same bill was a group called 'Heatwave' consisting of the duo Robert Casteneda and Triana Gonzalez. Heatwave played a blend of Latin and pop jazz and at the time were booked regularly at Serrano's Restaurant and La Palapa. Triana won 1st place in that years Austin Songwriters contest in the category of Best Foreign Song.

After 'Heatwave' came Wayne Hancock, opening for the event headliner Don Walser. At that time, Wayne was new to Austin having arrived in 1991. Wayne performed with his five-piece band and was billed around Austin as Wayne 'The Train' Hancock and The Honkey Tonk Breakmen. Waynes act included many obscure country and rock-a-billy gems and a few original songs. The Austin Chronicle said Wayne was 'carved from the stuff of Hank and Lefty'.

Don Walser was the event headliner that day. His set went from 5:15 to 5:45 and Bullfiddler wished his set could have been longer. Don had recently released his debut Watermelon album 'Rolling Stone from Texas', an album of genuine country & western and cowboy yodeling from 'the greatest country singer in the world,' as Lee Nichols of the Austin Chronicle described him. Don celebrated his 60th birthday that September and released his album with the help of Ray Benson of Asleep at The Wheel. Appearing with Don at that Rib Ticklin' event was steel guitar player Jimmy Day who had performed with Elvis Presley, Willie Nelson, Ray Price and was a member of the Country Music Hall of Fame. Don and his band the 'Pure Texas Band' was voted Best Country Band by the Music City Texas fanzine and Best Male Vocalist of the Year for two years in a row. Don said that "The old music really brings everyone together" and it did that hot summer evening. Don played regularly at Threadgill's on North Lamar and was also a regular at Jovitas on South First street. Don was originally from Lamesa, Texas and in his youth once shared a stage and billing with west Texan Buddy Holly.

During a thirty minute break ATCMHMR gave out it's awards for the best barbecue. After the awards ceremony Bullfiddlers band Los Downbeats played a forty minute set. The Rib Tickler booklet described the band: "Originally from El Paso, Texas, Los Downbeats have been described by The Austin Chronicle as 'a native Texas rock and roll band currently featuring songs from the 1920's and '30's. The performers in Los Downbeats were Bullfiddler on vocals and rhythm guitar, Jack David on sax and clarinet, Rick Lane on bass, Carol Simmons on piano and Bob Sarcinella on drums. Los Downbeats later performed that same set for the Hyde Park Tour of Homes, Eeyores Birthday Party, the Austin State Hospital and The State School. The bands members volunteered at Austin-Travis County MHMR activities while performing in busy other Austin bands. The following is Bullfiddler's set list with the songs and the song keys for that 45 minute set at Auditorium shores:

>Baby Face C
>Your Cheatin' Heart . . . C
>Wolly Bully . . . E
>The Sky is Cryin' . . . B
>Moonlight Bay Harvest Moon Medley . . . G
>Kwaligia . . . Dm
>Stormy Monday . . . . G
>My Baby's an Angel . . . A#
>Shake Rattle and Roll . . . C
>Just Because . . . C
>Townlake (Darktown) Strutters Ball . . . G
>Momma Don't Allow . . . G

 Closing out the show was Bullfiddlers old duet partner in The Raindogs, Tony Brussatt and The Jazz Pharaohs. Tony was becoming along with his successful jazz band. Tony and Bullfiddler reminisced back stage about their early gigs and memories of The Austin Outhouse. The Jazz Pharaohs were a five man band performing Tin Pan Alley songs from the twenties and thirties, occasionally spicing things up with some New Orleans jazz. The Jazz Pharaohs had been performing in Austin for three years and were regulars at the Elephant Room and Jazz on 6th Street. By 1994 The Jazz Pharaohs had released two independent cassettes: 'Jazz Pharaohs' and 'Tunes from the Tombs'. The band members included Tony Brussatt on vocals and guitar, Stanley 'Cool Pops' Smith on clarinet, Freddie Mendoza on trombone and vocals and Jeff Haley on stand-up bass and vocals. Tony, to hundreds of jazz aficionados eventually left Austin and took his confidence and talent with him but the Jazz Pharaohs continued to grow and develop in popularity.
 Bullfiddler could not sleep the night before that Auditorium Shores gig even though he was to began work at 7 am. He was so wired about being on the bill with those other musicians that he sat up all night and enjoyed an Austin sunrise. On one of these benefits in the late 1990's Tony Masarotti and The Downbeats opened for Tish Hinojosa at Auditorium Shores. Tish is a beloved bilingual diva from San Antonio, Texas who Bullfiddler met when she performed at The Old Reunion Building on the St. Edward's University Campus years earlier. An old handbill says that Tish's music "completely dissolves boundaries between cultures and language". On a roll those years Tish appeared on Austin City

Limits and CBS This Morning. At the Shores show she sold some copies of her recordings: Culture Swing and her 1995 release, Frontejas. Tish later that same year received Fox Televisions Bravo Honors award for her Frontejas album.

As for Los Downbeats, they were labeled as Tony and Los Downbeats. The write-up said that Anthony Locke was playing lead guitar but the press photo has James Merideth playing lead guitar with Tony Masaratti playing his red Gretch and Bullfiddler vigorously slapping his old bullfiddle. Tony and Los Downbeats played a forty minute rockabilly set that night on the same bill with Shelly King, the Salvation Day Parade, Urban Roots, Pete Ben and the Community Gospel Choir.

In 1994 Bullfiddler awoke one evening to find himself playing bass behind Kat Welch at Threadgill's 'Sittin' Singin' and Supper Sessions', then held every Wednesday night hosted by Champ Hood and the Threadgill Troubadours. Kat met Bullfiddler at Auditorium Shores and asked Bullfiddler if he would play with her on her first Threadgill's gig. It was Bullfiddlers first time to play at Threadgill's and to be associated with such a talented singer/musician/songwriter, Champ Hood. Later socially at Threadgill's Bullfiddler found and booked many acts for the annual ATCMHMR The Rib Tickler Affair. As Bullfiddler began to hang out regularly at Threadgill's he learned that many musicians were paid to play fundraiser gigs. They were paid out of the national Musicians Performance Trust Fund. This is a fund set up by the Musicians Union to cover musicians who played benefits for non-profit agencies. The band leader would fill out the paperwork and mail it into the union and a few months later, the musicians received their check for 'scale'. All of the major acts had to belong to the Musicians Union because they toured outside of Texas. Bullfiddler signed off on more than a few submission forms.

During the late 1990's karaoke became popular in Austin and numerous venues that formerly held open mics now bought and installed keroke machines. The advantage to karaoke is that anyone can sing along with the professionally pre-recorded music of their favorite songs without having to play an instrument themselves with the lyrics provided by a teleprompter. The bars paid less to a 'host' to run an open mic than they would have had to pay for a musician or a band to host an open mic, and once the PA levels were set, the sound levels remained consistent for the entire evening. In 1984 there were so many open mics that a budding serious songsmith could play his or her music on many different stages but after karaoke became popular, only two or three open mics flourished at first. There has since been a resurgence of acoustic and electric open mics all over Austin and surrounding hamlets.

Many of these modern day Austin open mics do not draw the crowds they did before the city wide no smoking ban went into effect. However, open mics outside Austin are doing well because there is no problem with indoor cigarette smoking, Poodies on 71, Sam's Town Point in Manchaca and The Oaks in Manor are fine examples of successful smokin' venues.

For two years Bullfiddler was assigned via ATCMHMR to spend an hour a day twice a week at Marbridge Ranch leading a 'music' class. Bullfiddlers supervisor loaned him a book on music therapy, showed Bullfiddler where the percussion instruments (tambourines, triangles and wood sticks) were located. For those two years Bullfiddler took a guitar and these percussion instruments out to Marbridge Ranch piano in the mess hall and conducted classes made up of elderly mild and moderately mentally retarded adults. The clients and Bullfiddler hit it off immediately and together they sang songs the elderly residents requested. These old Texans liked the old style country and western music and they sang with such enthusiasm that the Bullfiddler and Marbridge Ranch staff decided to record an album (cassette tape) of songs of the residents choosing. The project was recorded and released to the Marbridge Ranch community right before Christmas, 1991. Many of the group proudly sent copies home to loved ones. This was their chosen set list:

I'll Fly Away
When The Saints go Marching In
My Bonnie
Your Cheatin' Heart
Lovesick Blues
Love Me Tender
The Eyes of Texas
Amazing Grace
Baby Face
Jambalaya
Commin' Round the Mountain

A photo of the residents was on the cover and needless to say, both the clients and the staff were delighted with their tangible product. The following year the residents recorded a Christmas album of their favorite Christmas songs. After the taping for the Christmas project was done Bullfiddler had the idea of raising the tape speed so that the singers sounded like chipmunks. The tape speed plan was accomplished with the help of a tape machine with variable speeds the Bullfiddler borrowed from the Texas School for the Blind. The clients liked the idea and together they released "Peace on Earth; Christmas Songs—Chipmunk Style" in 1992. The cassette was released just in time for Christmas. The songs were mutually chosen by the group after singing through numerous songs during the weekly music therapy sessions.

Bullfiddlers affiliation with the Hyde Park Methodist Church led him to play the annual Hyde Park Tour of Homes gigs. Each year the Hyde Park Neighborhood Association had a fair at the Elizabet Ney Museum and conducted tours of some of the older neighborhood homes. The Bullfiddler was hired to put a period piece band together playing music from the 1920's and he was lucky enough to find Stanley Smith who played clarinet and Boomer Norman on guitar. Bullfiddler played his bullfiddle and as a trio they would wear striped shirts, Derbys while playing on a front porch of one of the older turn-of-the-century homes. As Los Downbeats they played the Hyde Park gig for four consecutive years.

Another of ATCMHMR's annual music events was Eeyore's Birthday Party. The agency set up the children's area and booked the children's concert at Poohs Corner. The agency asked Bullfiddler who was gaining booking experience with the Auditorium Shores projects to help book the Eeyore's children's show. The show was made up of story tellers, musicians, magicians and jugglers. Bullfiddler booked the Eeyore's Children's Show for six years with such singers as Patty Finney singing children's songs, Carol Zweeb, a storyteller, Tony Maxaroni whose specialty was blowing up children's balloons and shaping the balloons into animals with a children's comedy sketch, the U.T. Juggling Society and of course, Los Downbeats with Janice Goodspeed and Maribet Gradzier bellydancing to the music. The Eeyore's communal drumming eventually became so loud and when the drum circle moved right behind Poohs Corner the show was canceled. A children's show just could not compete with three to four hundred plus percussionists.

Of the many benefits of music therapy is the promotion of physical activity and interaction clients have with their peers. At both the Austin State Hospital with the mentally ill and with ATCMHMR with the mentally retarded one could see the positive effects of music therapy up close. There are wallflowers in all walks of life and more so in the mental health world. When a good lively band begins playing music almost immediately clients would begin moving parts of their bodies to the rhythm. The wallflowers would gradually come off the wall, step out of their shell and get some moderate physical exercise while moving to the rhythm and interacting with each other. The behaviors were the same whether playing at Neo's at the Austin State School, a MHMR campout or in the gym at the Austin State Hospital. There was never any trouble during Bullfiddlers gigs, only lots of smiles on sweaty faces. Active group participation was evident with the two tapes recorded at Marbridge Ranch where one could see a little older country woman from Dime Box Texas singing cheek-to-cheek with an former upper-class Dallasite.

Bullfiddler's divorce became final in 1994 while he was living on Franklin Avenue. Bullfiddler had an old upright piano sitting on his front porch and he began to play it daily while going through the divorce. By playing piano Bullfiddler learned all the chords on his right hand and the corresponding bass patterns with his left. Within two or three months after the divorce was final and porch piano pounding came to an end, Bullfiddler could play piano by ear and played all the songs he personally knew on guitar or bass. He sold the piano to an elderly man who lived half a block down the street on the other side of Wallar Creek. The neighbors got quite a hoot watching the old man and a friend push that piano down Franklin street and into the old man's apartment. The old gentleman insisted on giving Bullfiddler $50.00 even though he was told he could have the piano for free for just hauling it off.

At the turn of the decade music could be heard up and down Franklin Avenue and in many other neighborhoods. One day the Austin City Council came up with some seed money for the Austin music industry. If someone could form a music business that could hire three or more people full-time they could get grant money to start a music related business. Consequently rehearsal halls opened up like petunias all around Austin. The rehearsal rooms each came equipped with a new PA system, a technician to keep the gear running, a secretary to make appointments a janitorial crew and an accountant. Rehearsal complexes became big business especially when the Austin Police Department became involved. APD began visiting home band rehearsals weather there was a noise complaint or not warning the musicians that on the next visit there could be a fine or worse. Many musicians smoked pot and did other drugs, so they were compelled to rent rehearsal space in the local rehearsal halls, fearing a citation or least or a drug bust. Franklin Avenue as with the rest of the 'hood' became quiet almost over night. When Muller Airport closed down along with the lack of jet noises and band practices, the atmosphere was very eerie indeed. One could walk their dog at sunset and not hear a note or the sound of a jet plane.

Within a year after Bullfiddlers divorce he met again and became involved with Leti de la Vega for what was to be an exciting and personally rewarding bilingual Austin musical adventure. Leti and the Bullfiddler had met in the mid 80's at a jam in Leti's living room at her house on Mary street in South Austin. Tony Brassatt and the Bullfiddler jammed along with or listened to Jubal Clark, Blaze Foley and Towns Van Zandt. The day after that jam session Leti and Bullfiddler had one eventful date. The transmission in Bullfiddlers Chevy six cylinder truck would occasionally lock up and on Bullfiddlers date with Leti his transmission locked up in the middle of Barton Springs road. Bullfiddler had to get out of the truck, climb underneath and unhook the linkage. With greasy hands Leti and Bullfiddler ended up watching a Willie Nelson taping an Austin City Limits show at the University of Texas. That evening Bullfiddler took Leti to her house on Mary street and again met Blaze and Leti's brother Richard de la Vega. Richard was playing bass for Blaze at that time while Bullfiddler was playing his bullfiddle with the Raindogs. On their second meeting years later in 1995 Leti played some family songs she was working on using a beat up no-name guitar with rusty steel strings and high action. Bullfiddler played some bass that night and they immediately teamed up to co-write and produce two CD original bi-lingual CD projects.

Leti was given an Alvarez guitar with lite gage strings and yet her fingers continued to bleed from all the obsessive work Leti put in to learning how to play guitar. Coming from a family of roofers, she had a strong work ethic and knew the value of developing callouses on her fingertips. The was proud of them. Leti finally got to where she could sing without looking at her chording hand and the guitar was set-up with an electric pick-up that was installed by Walter Hutchinson at Walter's Musical Exchange on North Loop.

Chapter 17

BLAZE FOLEY

Blaze Foley was one of the most interesting singer songwriters Bullfiddler had the pleasure to know and work with. The two first met at Leti's South Austin living room and later at The Austin Outhouse. They began to talk to each other when Blaze came in to the Austin Outhouse one day after having recovered two boxes of his first album. The vinal album was recorded in Muscle Shoals but was confiscated by Federal narcotics agents. According to Blaze the album was funded with proceeds from some drug activity that Blaze had nothing to do with. He had been playing for some of these drug dealers and they liked his music so much that some drug proceeds funded a full-blown recording session with the Muscle Shoals All-Star Horn Section. When the drug bust came down, Blazes' albums, hot off the press were confiscated by federal agents. After much cajoling the feds finally released two boxes of the album to Blaze. He used those albums in Austin to pay for taxi rides, bar tabs, and with Bullfiddler as collateral for a five dollar loan. Blaze later offered to buy the album back, but Bullfiddler refused the offer and found himself playing bass for Blaze at The Outhouse when Blaze' other bass player, Richard de la Vega was in Colorado.

On one particular show at The Outhouse Bullfiddler asked Blaze if he could sing one of Bullfiddler's original songs during the break. Blaze gave the OK. Bullfiddler then asked Blaze during the intermission if he could use some of Blazes tape duct tape. Blaze was a duct tape fanatic and used that tape to repair and cover everything from sport coats to boots.

"What's it for?" Blaze asked.

"So I can tape the lyric sheet to the microphone stand," Bullfiddler said.

"Tell you what," Blaze said as he looked Bullfiddler right in the eyes, 'why don't you wait until you know the song before you sing it?"

Bullfiddler walked out to the back yard, smoked some with friends and fumed at not being able to sing the song. Bullfiddler had another set to do with Blaze so he calmed down and did the set, admitting to himself that Blaze was right. He could sing the song with more passion if he knew it in his heart.

During the middle of the second set Blaze told the story about the man with the Cadillac convertible and his three penguin friends:

"There was a man driving a white Cadillac convertible down North Lamar. In the back seat he had three penguins. The driver drove past McDonald's where an Austin motorcycle cop was sitting on his bike eating a hamburger. Seeing the car and the penguins the cop threw his sandwich down, chased after the Cadillac and pulled the car over in front of the Hole in the Wall.

"What in the hell have you got here? The cop asked.

"These are my three penguin friends. We're just out for a cruise".

"Well, take them to the zoo right now', the cop ordered the driver.

"Yes sir', the man replied as he drove off without getting a ticket.

The following day, the cop being a creature of habit was again at McDonald's when he spotted the man and his Cadillac again driving down North Lamar toward town. Once again the cop, threw his sandwich to the ground and sped after the car. When he pulled the Cadillac over once again a block north of the Hole in the Wall the cop noticed that the man and the three penguins were all wearing sunglasses.

"What's going on here"? The cop asked the driver. "I thought I told you to take those penguins to the zoo".

"I did", said the man. "Today we are going to the beach". Bullfiddler could not stay mad at a man who not only made sense but also had a sense of humor.

A few months later Blaze was shot and killed in a house on Mary street a few doors down from Leti's place. Apparently Blaze had befriended an elderly gentleman and one day the old man's son came home and demanded money from the old man. Blaze interfered and suggested the younger man 'get a job'. The old man's son went into a bedroom, returned with a rifle and shot Blaze once in the chest, killing him instantly. Blaze died on that South Austin living room floor and the assailant, the old man's son was later no billed by an Austin grand jury. Bullfiddler dashed off a letter to the Austin Chronicle about Blaze, and the newspaper published it as Blaze' obituary.

Before Leti de la Vega and Bullfiddler began recording Bullfiddler was booked to do some studio work with a mutual south Austin friend, Whitey Ray Huitt. An Austin native, Whitey was very popular in Austria and Germany and toured Europe once or twice a year. He rarely played any gigs in Austin, preferring to lay out and catch his breath. It was through an introduction to Whitey by Leti that Bullfiddler was able to record on Whitey's album 'Austex

Blues', named after an old Austin bar the Austex Lounge. Bullfiddler played on two songs on the project along with such Austin notables as Floyd Domino on piano, Robert Asocar on violin, Appa Perry, (well known 6th street blues bass player and host), Spencer Perskin, the founder of Shiva's Headband on violin and Danny Hawk on guitar. The musicians rarely met in the studio, each coming in on their own and laying down their track to what had been previously recorded. The recording came out under Chewahwah Chase Records.

In the summer of 1996 when Bullfiddler was buying his home on Waller Creek in Austin. Whitey invited him to play bass with him in Europe. Having just bought his creekside house, Bullfiddler turned him down. Bullfiddler also turned down Whitey's offer to tour Europe when Bullfiddler saw photos of Whitey's previous German gigs. There were photos of Whitey playing in a bar in downtown Berlin with a Confederate flag hanging behind the stage. Bullfiddler developed a vision problem in that he could not see a Texas Jewboy bullfiddling in a Berlin redneck bar. Leti and Bullfiddler later began recording their second CD in George Coyne's Parrot Tracks Studio in Manchuria, Texas.

Leti de la Vega is a bilingual songwriter/singer and their first musical project was recording her family's original Spanish language songs. On that project the two co-wrote one song, 'Bluebonnet Highway'. The bilingual recording was done in the BNL Revue studio, Elk Audio with Eve Keniansky engineering the project. Ponty Bone played his hot accordion on some songs and Ron Erwin played his snare drum. Geoff Outlaw, co-star with Ario Guthrie in the cult movie 'Alice's Restaurant' played mandolin on one of the songs even though he was at that time in the process of getting a friendly divorce from Leti. Spencer Perkin and Champ Hood shared fiddle projects on the project. Together Leti and Bullfiddler released the recording and all rights to that project were later bought and re-released by Austin's Deep South Productions. On the re-mix Leti re-sang some of her vocals, improving the project greatly.

Leti and the Bullfiddler had their first live performance with Calvin Russell on the bill at Paul Sessums Black Cat annex on Red River in downtown Austin. Calvin later did two duets with Leti on their first project now entitled 'La Primavera'. Years earlier Calvin signed with the French label 'New Rose' after he was released from his second stint in a Texas prison. The French idolized Calvin and he released numerous albums and well-done videos on the New Rose Label. Leti had made custom tee shirts for Calvin Russell at a tee-shirt shop she worked for part-time. Calvin was one of the first to work on Leti's and Bullfiddlers project, singing duets with Leti.

Their first guest on their first recording was Teye a Danish gypsy flamenco guitarist who was currently playing with Joe Ely. Ely discovered Teye in Europe and brought him to Austin. Teye later organized his own show with his vibrant Spanish gypsy guitar playing while his wife and two other women danced in Spanish costumes. As Teye played his fierce Gypsy rhythms his wife and her girlfriends danced on wooden floors, tapping out rhythms with their wooden high heeled black shoes. In the recording studio Teye wanted to do take after take on the same song, and Bullfiddler had to firmly cut him off. Bullfiddler explained to Teye that Teye wasn't paying for the studio time and in Bullfiddlers opinion Teye had nailed the track on his second take, which he did with perfection.

Chapter 18

CHAMP'S PIANO

In contrast to the gruff Teye, Champ Hood was as innovative and humble a musician as one could ever expect to work with in a recording studio. Champ always had a warm smile and was chock full of innovative musical ideas. He recorded a number of fiddle tracts on both of Leti's and Bullfiddlers recordings. Champ would listen to the tracks and he would invent wonderful instrumentation that fit the song perfectly. Champ later invited Leti and Bullfiddler to perform at Threadgill's 'Sitting' Singing' Supper' sessions that he and the Troubadours hosted every Wednesday night. During the recording of their first project Bullfiddler and Leti visited Champ at Champ's home to give him some song charts. The Bullfiddler played some on Champs old upright piano.

"If you want it, you can have it," Champ said.

"Seriously?", Bullfiddler asked.

"If you can get it out of here you can have it," Champ said.

Bullfiddler backed up a red Mazda truck to the front porch and together they pushed the upright out the front door and easily onto the truck. Champ refused to take any money and when Bullfiddler and Leti pulled up to Bullfiddler's front door Bullfiddler was sure they would have to take off the door to get the piano inside the house. To their amazement the piano was gently lifted through the front entrance without having to do any remodeling. Bullfiddler invited a piano tuner over and the old man immediately sat down and began working on the piano without talking cost specifics or materials. The old piano tuner charged a hundred dollars and for a few years that piano stayed in 'pretty good' tune. It is little things like that, the ease in which Bullfiddler relocated the piano, or the making of all green lights when driving the piano home that lead him to believe that a higher power must be at work in Bullfiddlers life. The piano was just meant to happen'.

'Rancho Vallejo, Mexico' was for Leti and Bullfiddler a major co-writing experience. Leti is her family historian and she and Bullfiddler often took care packages of clothes and food to her small family ranch in Mexico near Harlingen, Texas. The two always played an acoustic set when visiting the Mexican ranch. On one warm evening Leti and Bullfiddler played outside in front of a small grocery store in the central part of Los Indios, Mexico. Leti and Bullfiddler were that evening a minor international sensation. The people in Los Indios loved Leti.

Together Leti and Bullfiddler would come up with an aspect of her family's history or the history of the family ranch and compose a bilingual song around the topic. Often the two took what they laughingly called 'working vacations', going to the Texas coast or to the Dabbs Hotel, an old railroad inn in Llano with the objective of writing and coming back to Austin with a complete song. In this manner Leti and Bullfiddler wrote six of the eleven songs that appeared on their second CD.

The second project was recorded entirely at Parrot Tracks Studios and while recording the music, Leti and Bullfiddler made some videos for Hank Sinatra. Hank was famous around Austin for his excellent coverage of the Austin music scene and on his Austin Access TV show Hank had the likes of Towns Van Zandt, Blaze Foley, hundreds of Austin songwriters and Leti. She had fun inviting friends to do session work in the Parrot Tracks Recording Studio. The two gladly paid some of the musicians while others wouldn't take a dime. On this project along with Champ Hood on fiddle and background vocals was Champs co-host at Thread gills, Marvin Dykhaus. Marvin was very busy those days, playing regularly with Tish Hinojosa, often going overseas. Playing percussion on that project was John 'Mombo' Treanor. John was another of those rare humble Austin musicians who was loved by everyone he ever came in contact with. John also played with Tony Price at her 'Happy Hippy Hour' at the Continental Club, with Marcia Ball and on occasion with Doak Short or Ponty Bone. Mombo often took road kill home and fashioned it into hats and for this skill and his superior percussion he was written up often in the local Austin newspapers. Mombo received his share of rave reviews for his recordings and performances.

While Leti was working her part-time job at the tee shirt factory she had a referral to the Continental Club regular, Toni Price. Leti designed and printed tee shirts to advertise Toni's newest album. While on a delivery to Toni's apartment with two boxes of shirts Leti asked Toni if she could play a guitar that sat in the corner of her living room. Leti played and sang her brother Richard de la Vega's song 'Old Fiddlers Waltz' and Toni was so taken with the song that she later recorded it and placed the song first on her 'Sol Power' album. Leti's brother Richard began receiving royalty checks while living with his bride in Colorado, usually two or three hundred fifty dollars each check. While hanging around the Continental Club Bullfiddler and Leti invited Doak Short to sing two duets with Leti on their project. Doak came into the studio twice and sang on cuts 2,4 and 9. Leti also had her mother, daughter and granddaughter add backing vocals on many of the songs.

Somewhere along the way a local South Austin record company, Deep South Productions bought out the second project while Leti and Bullfiddler were recording at Parrot Tracks Studio. Deep South finished paying for the recording and mixing the masters to "Rancho Viejo, Mexico" and released it in 2001. On their second CD entitled 'Rancho Viejo Mexico', Leti and Bullfiddler wrote and arranged six of the eleven bilingual songs. They are '500 Horses', 'Shooting Star', "Recipes of the Ancestors', 'Cemetery Song', 'Los Vaqueros' and 'Water Girls'.

The following appeared on the "Rancho Viejo' project: Leti on vocals, guitar and rainstick, her mother Eustolia on vocals, her daughter Suzzette Johnson on vocals, her grand daughter Eustolia on vocals, her brother Leo on guitar, Goeff Outlaw on guitar and mandolin, Marvin Dykhaus on guitar and mandolin, Champ Hood on fiddle, Fernando Castillo on trumpet, T. Hale on bass, George Coyne on heartbeat, kitchen and wind sounds, Eddie Painter on drums and concertina, John 'Mombo' Treanor on drums, Rachel Rain on vocals, Ginnie Powell on vocals and Doak Short on vocals. Bulllfiddler played acoustic and electric bass on six songs and rhythm guitar on four songs.

Leti's first CD, now titled 'La Primavera' had been re-released by Deep South in 1997 with Fernando Castillo of Del Castillo playing trumpet on one of the songs. Geoff Outlaw played guitar and mandolin on two songs. For some reason or another, when it came time to sign the paperwork for the two projects over to Deep South and Leti, Bullfiddler put a '0' in the percentage blanks. If it wasn't for Leti Bullfiddler might never have had the opportunity to work with some of Austin's best musicians. The music is now selling well on the Internet and at some of Leti's rare shows. The Bullfiddler was paid with wonderful musical experiences and made good friends in the Austin music world. Bullfiddler still thought of what it would be like if he knew how to read music.

It is interesting how relationships between singer-songwriters in Austin interweave with each other. The one song that Whitey Ray Huitt wrote that Bullfiddler felt compelled to learn is a song called 'The Man'. It is the story of two Austin singer-songwriters and their ill-fated trip to New York City. Whitey had a close friend in the 1970's, one Jubal Clark, a lyrical troubadour who was described by Whitey as "a guiding light for Austin's aspiring singer-songwriters".

Bullfiddler had the good fortune to play bass behind Jubal twice, once at a residence on Mary street in South Austin and once during a recording project at the Austin Outhouse in 1993. Jubal died Saturday, May 17th, 1997 at the age of 68 in his apartment from prostate cancer. He was part of a hard-living clan of Austin singer-songwriters who frequented clubs such as Spellman's, Emmajoe's, the Austex Lounge and the Austin Outhouse. It is safe to say that Jubal will be remembered more for his influence on other songwriters than his recording career. When Bullfiddler knew Jubal, Jubal had no recording career, but a close friend of his, Lost John Casner did record some of Jubals music and helped Jubal get one of his songs 'Love Stealer' recorded by Calvin Russell. Calvin Russell, Jubal Clark, Whitey Ray Huitt and Blaze Foley could be remembered as early cornerstones of the Austin country and folk scenes.

Larry Monroe said that Jubal was one of those "authentic guys like Blaze and Townes for whom being a songwriter meant everything to them. They lived their songs." At the time of his death Jubal was working on a recording project, 'Gypsy Cowboy' with John Casner. The posthumous CD features songs Jubal had studio recorded in 1990 and some tracks recorded live at the Austin Outhouse in 1993.

Chapter 19

WILLIE'S PICNIC

One of Jubal's last performances was at a Willie Nelson picnic in Lukenbach in 1993. By that time Jubal had played several previous picnics and also appeared in some of Nelson's films such as the role of a horse thief in "Red Headed Stranger'.

Bullfiddler had the honor of 'working' at one of Willie's picnics in 1994. He arrived at the picnic grounds the night before the concert driving his blue and white Volkswagen van along his dog. The smell of barbecue and beer and marijuana was thick in the air as Bullfiddler drove down a bumpy dusty road. He was given a blue picnic tee shirt by security and allowed to sleep on the grounds directly behind the stage, falling asleep later that July fourth evening to the sweet smell of mesquite. Earlier that night he worked as a gopher, setting up tables backstage, fetching stuff and later the next afternoon worked a three hour shift directing traffic where to park on picnic day. Before the end of his shift a Bandito on his motorcycle drove up to Bullfiddler with a car full of people behind him. They all knew each other. When Bullfiddler tried to direct the biker and his friends to their parking spot eighteen rows behind the stage, the Bandito told Bullfiddler with a friendly attitude that he didn't want to leave his bike all the way out "in the sticks".

"I am only doing what I was told to do," Bullfiddler said.

"Do you smoke dope?" the biker asked.

"Sometimes," Bullfiddler said.

"Do you drink?" the Bandito asked.

"On occasion," Bullfiddler said.

"Tell you what," the Bandito said," we'll give you a six pack of Budwiser and a joint if you let us through".

Bullfiddler saw that the biker was wearing his Bandito colors and took the joint and the beer. Bullfiddler was going to 'cop a buzz' for the picnic. When Bullfiddlers shift was over he saw the biker along with over fifty or so Banditos back stage. They were part of the 'informal security' Willie had often used and that hot summer night there was no trouble. The weather was very dry and over one hundred dry degrees with dust constantly blowing in the air. The Willie tee shirt not only allowed Bullfiddler backstage but also into the free food and beverage tent. For that one night Bullfiddler saw what the in-crowd was like and how they behaved as Willie and others on the bill that night talked casually and ate backstage. The smell of marijuana was everywhere and once again Bullfiddler was amazed at how well cowboys and hippies got along.

Willie told some funny stories that night on that flat dusty field. One of his stories was about a man who was in his apple orchard with a pig. The man held the pig up by the pigs hind legs and the pig pulled apples off one of the trees with his mouth. A man was walking down the road and stopped to watch the action. He told the farmer pig that it must have taken some time to teach the pig to do that. The farmer replied: "time don't mean nothin' to a pig'.

Willie went on to point out that both political parties are going to have to agree to pass a farm bill. Factory farms, Willie explained are the worst things that can be done to people, the environment and the publics general health. The dangers are there, he explained including diseases that may or may not be harmful to humans. "Either way, it's easier for small family farmers to insure a healthier climate on the farm because there a few pigs on acres of ground and a variety of products spread over several acres, not a hundred thousand pigs in a pen next to a retirement home in the country.

Willie told of the time when while on the bus a band member was wearing some real spiffy boots.

"Fine boots there, where'd you get them?" one of Willies bandmates asked.

"Mexico', the man answered.

Another man in the band said that in Mexico they treat leather in human urine. Then one of the band members came up with the idea of storing the bands urine on the band bus, stockpiling it in Abbott and selling it to cattlemen. Another band member thought that was a bad idea.

"We outta just piss on the cows and sell the hides as pre-treated leather".

Chapter 20

THE GREAT JESSIE TAYLOR

Jessie Taylor was a pleasure to play music in public with. Besides playing a gig with Jessie at the original skinny Black Cat Lounge, Bullfiddler had the pleasure to also play bass with Jessie at both the Austin State Hospital and at CB Stubbefields bar. For a town with a lot of guitar pickers, Jessie was the "most ferocious". At the Black Cat gig they were paid $40.00 each and after the gig Paul Sessums bought Jessie Taylor, Curley, Tony Masaratti and Bullfiddler all the pizza they could eat. At the State Hospital gigs Jessie sat in and played rockabilly lead guitar with Tony and the Tigers, playing his heart out for those in the State Hospital. He offered to play for free but he was forced to accept ten dollars for the hour-long gig.

Born in Lubbock, Texas Jessie was part of a group of Lubbock musicians that lit up Austin. Jessie played for years with Joe Ely as they toured with the Clash who nicknamed him Jessie "Guitar" Taylor. Bullfiddler first saw Jessie playing with Tommy Hancock and The Supernatural Family Band at the Shorthorn Lounge on north Lamar. Jessie also played with Ponty Bone and Loyd Maines and recorded with the Maines Brothers on their first album the brothers recorded while growing up together in Lubbock, Texas.

Jessie was 55 when he died of Hepatitis-C in 2006. Keith Richards and Jessie got along so well that Joe Ely and Jessie opened for some Stones shows out in California. According to Stubbs, Jessie was the first white musician to play at Stubbs BBQ in Lubbock on east Broadway Avenue. The Lubbock-born musicians friendship with CB Stubbefield led Jessie to jam on many of the regular Lubbock open mic jams. Some of these jams included Stevie Ray Vaughn, Jimmie Dale Gilmore, Ponty Bone, and just about every musician in Lubbock. Jessie was in Jimmy Dale Gilmore's first band, the T-Nickle House Band. Those Sunday open mics continued when Stubbs moved to Austin. On his arrival in Austin

Stubbs sold BBQ out of Antone's blues club on Guadalupe Street, but after two years CB leased his last BBQ joint on Austin's I-35 access road. Stubbs held those Sunday jams where Bullfiddler often saw and occasionally played bass behind Jessie. Bullfiddler sat in with new friends and old strangers at Stubbs often while producer Hank Sinatra videotaped over 22 consecutive weeks of blues and rhythm and blues at the club. Before ME television Austinites could see some of those videos on the old Austin Music Network and everyone who had a guitar knew of bot Jessie Taylor and Hank Sinatra.

Jessie was a Golden Gloves boxer with large tattooed biceps, nobody wanted to mess with Jessie. In all their years of touring and recording together, Jessie and Joe Ely never had a major argument. Joe said that Jessie was a total 'sweetheart'. Joe told of a time when he and Jessie were playing a New Years' Eve dance in Lubbock. A Bandito threw a string of firecrackers at Jessie's feet. Jessie challenged and then laid out the Bandito on the Lubbock dance floor with just one left hook.

The last time Bullfiddler saw Jessie play was three weeks before Stubbs closed. Jessie was always the kind of guy that would talk to anyone; fans mobbed him one night at Threadgill's while he and Bullfiddler talked about Jessies upcoming one-man art show. Jessie did not play music that night but Champ Hood announced that Jessie was having his exhibit of his artwork at Laughing at The Sun Gallery in South Austin. Jessie was an original member of the Flatlanders and performed at Threadgill's North often. He even jammed once on one song with BNL Revue.

BNL Revue let many friends sit in on their gigs at Ruby's BBQ and The Green Mesquite. Often BNL Revue went out to open mics to practice new songs and gage audience reaction. One of the most cantankerous open mic hosts was Ken Schaffer who often sponsored various versions of his "Safety in Numbers' showcases. Ken's attitude towards his fellow songwriters was worn on his sleeve often and in the mid-1990's he had a habit of not showing to emcee the show. He was known for refusing to let certain musicians sign up and perform. The last place Ken hosted his Safety in Numbers Showcase was at a little Mexican food-bar that was located on 290 east of Highland Mall. Ken ran an ad for a BNL Revue's Showcase in John Conquest's widely read Music City Texas News. The only problem with the ad was that it did not mention what night BNL was going to perform and Ken did not provide a telephone number. Anyone interested in BNL Revue had to look up the club or call the band.

During that same period, Eve Keniansky while mixing an album asked Bullfiddler if he wanted to go on a photo shoot with her on 6th street. Bullfiddler grabbed his bullfiddle and together they met two hundred Austin musicians standing in the street in front of a music store called Local Flavor. Local Flavor only sold music that was written or recorded in Austin, specializing and supporting native Texans. The store was selling the BNL Revue cassette and together Eve, Bullfiddler and the other musicians ranging from punk to country posed for a photo in front of Local Flavor. The photo was published without a cut line but if one looks closely they might recognize Emily Kaitz, Tony Brassatt, Toni Price and Wayne the Train Hancock. The photo took up half a page of the Music City News and John Conquest was one of two writers to review BNL Revue's work. The reviews were favorable but not gushing.

Three BNL Revue musicians, Eve, Mike Ochs and Bullfiddler played one night at an open mic at the non-smoking Cactus Cafe and Bar on the University of Texas Campus. The air was pure with an occasional whiff of perfume floating about the small room. BNL Revue could only perform three songs which they ran through quickly as the band humbly tried to promote their just released cassette recording. During this period in the late 1990's four members of BNL, Eve, Mike, Georgina (on tenor sax) and Bullfiddler played a couple of gigs for a belly dancing friend of Eves, Zerehade who put on shows at the original Ruta Maya on West 4th street. BNL Revue played background instrumental music while Zerhade and her girlfriends performed their belly dancing show. This reminded Bullfiddler of the New Years Eve gig in that Juarez strip joint, only everyone was much more civilized. The music was richer, the acts were more 'artistic' and the coffee was French. It was at Ruta Maya that Leti de la Vega and Bullfiddler were asked to play for Max Nofziger's 50th birthday party.

Leti had a camera that night, an Instamatic and Max's parents asked her to take photos and mail them to them which she did. Max was an Austin City Councilman at the time and known to be quite a character. His parents were average middle class nice people. Most musicians at that time played for fundraisers for Max who when eventually elected to Austin City Council quickly lost interest in politics. To Max' credit he did nothing illegal nor did he sponsor any major legislation that had a lasting impact on Austin. His parties however were always a blast for friends and musicians could either play music or eat and drink.

During Bullfiddlers tenure with BNL Revue he was introduced to a quaint upstairs coffee house and performance venue, the Chicago House. During the 1980's and 90's The Chicago House was run by two very nice women, Peg Miller and Glynda Cox. For a brief period Bullfiddler played not only with BNL Revue but with Mike Ochs and his friend Shemp on Mike's original songs. The Chicago House put on live music, small plays and poetry slams. It was there that Bullfiddler first heard the term poetry slam and saw his first slam at Chicago House. He came away very impressed because unlike the stale poetry readings he witnessed in El Paso beat joints where the poet took the stage opened their book or papers and read their poetry with a monotone delivery, these poets had their poetry memorized and recited it with theatrics and passion, without music and with a wide range of various body language. This was poetry taken to a theatrical level and the one poet who made a lasting impression on Bullfiddler was a guy everyone called Whammo. Bullfiddler later watched as Whammo and the original Asylum Street Spankers developed their act at the Outhouse.

The Chicago House provided Bullfiddler the opportunity to get his feelings hurt. An locally famous Austin woman who wrote humorous well received songs was always friendly to Bullfiddler whenever he had his bullfiddle with him. She would then talk nice to Bullfiddler and then ask him if she could play a song of hers on his bullfiddle during her set. One night Bullfiddler left his bullfiddle at home and visited the Chicago House. The songwriter was scheduled to perform and did not so much as say 'Hi' to the sensitive Bullfiddler. Bullfiddler felt at the time that the only reason she ever talked to him was so she could use his Kay bullfiddle.

Jimmy LaFave was a regular at the Chicago House as was Wayne the Train Hancock and other now well-known Austinites. Glenda and Peg respected the working and striving musicians but without falling into that smug self-congratulation thing that at times has been so toxic to the Austin music scene. Songwriting and the performing arts was always front and center with those two. Glynda Cox died January 23, 2008 but the warm memories of the Chicago House will stay with many Austin musicians for a long time.

Playing bass in Austin has led to some of Bullfiddlers memorable gigs. One of the most exciting was the gig with Toni Price and Leti De La Vega at the Laughing at The Sun Art Gallery in south Austin. The Gallery had a Winter Solstice program to present the artwork and musical performances by Leti and other artists.

The show happened on the night of December 21, 1994 at the gallery on 2209 S. 1st street. Leti displayed and sold various painted and embroidered fabrics and their CD. The musical part of the show was provided by Toni Price who opened the show with her "Oceanic Poems'. Playing her music was her band from The Continental Club, Champ Hood, Scrappy Jud Newcomb and Casper Rawls. In the second set, Leti performed her bilingual music featuring a newly written song about a contested family Spanish land grant. Leti and Bullfiddler played that set with Geoff Outlaw, Eve Kuniansky, Eddie Painter.

ARRRIBA, the Hispanic arts and business Austin newspaper called Leti "an artist, clothing and jewelry designer, songwriter, and historian who often performs at the Threadgill's North Austin location". Once again, playing music with her was Champ Hood, a highlight in Leti's musical life. Eddie Painter, a multi-talented musician played drums with Leti and Bullfiddler on that gig as well as on her recordings. Eddie also recorded with Diamond Simon and the Roughcuts before branching off to work on his own Greatful Dead oriented musical projects.

Performing with Geoff Outlaw was eerie in that Bullfiddler had helped Leti obtain a no-fault divorce from Geoff just three months before the Laughing at the Sun Gallery. There were no hard feelings and Geoff accompanied Leti and her fellow musicians on mandolin, performing like the pro that he is. Geoffrey Bowie Outlaw was listed in the Austin Chronicle as "a folk-oriented blues and country musician with thirty-one years in the biz. Geoff formerly played with the Fugs, Hedy West, Rosalie Sorrells and for eleven years with Arlo Guthrie. In the past Geoff often played gigs around Austin with Leti and her brother Richard. Everyone playing music that night was honored to back Geoff as he sang Johnny Cash's "Hey Porter". Champ played an amazing fiddle break, swapping licks with Geoff's mandolin. With heavy incense in the air the musicians rehearsed "Hey Porter" only minutes before going on at the Laughing at The Sun Gallery.

Chapter 21

BILINGUAL TEXAS MUSIC

The first album Leti de la Vega and Bullfiddler recorded was a first for each of them. Leti and Bullfiddler arranged the thirteen songs, twelve of which were original de la Vega family songs. The personnel on that project consisted of some well-known Austin musicians. There was Leti on vocals, percussion and rhythm guitar, Ponty Bone on accordion, Leti's mother Eustolia on vocals, Leti's grandbaby Eustolia on vocals, Leti's brother Leo de la Vega on lead and rhythm guitars and vocals, Ron Erwin on percussion, Champ Hood on acoustic guitar and violin, Eve Kuniansky on mandolin, flute, recorder percussion, harmonica, backing vocals and alto sax, Eddie Painter on percussion and concertina, Spencer Perskin on violin, Calvin Russell on vocals, Teye Wintjerp on classical guitar, Ponty Bone on accordion and Tye-Dye John Williamson on acoustic bass.

This recording was first released in 1996. On the CE appeared Leti's and Bullfiddlers first co-written song along with Leti's brother Richards original 'The Old Fiddler's Waltz'.

It was an humbling honor for Bullfiddler to record with Ponty Bone. Ponty was one of those one or two take musicians who always gave his best. When Ponty came into the studio to add accordion to the songs, all he had to do was listen to the song once or twice, look at the chart and then add his own version of what he thought would work on his accordion.

Ponty Bone was no stranger to the Austin recording world. He began playing accordion at age five and in the sixties he made his first album while playing regular gigs at Austin's Vulcan Gas Company. He toured internationally during the seventies and eighties with Joe Ely and since then has split his time between recording and playing with his own bands, the Squeezetones and Zydeco Loco. Ponty has also recorded with Jimmie Dale Gilmore, Timbuck3, The Supernatural

Family Band, the Texana Dames and many others. Because of his association with Ponty during the recording sessions Bullfiddler was able to work once again with Ponty during the summer of 1995. Bullfiddler was fortunate to book both Ponty Bone and the Squeezetones and the Texana Dames to play on the same bill at Auditorium Shores for an ATCMHMR benefit.

Charlene Hancock, Traci Lamar and Connie Hancock formed the nucleus of a band whose musical mastery ranged from classical country to Cajun, R&B, polkas, conjunto, salsa and rock 'n' roll with a strong core of original material. In 1994 the Texana Dames released their first recording in Europe but they along with their leader, Tommy Hancock will be remembered as some of the best music Lubbock had to offer. John X Reed played lead guitar on that Auditorium Shores gig, and Ponty sat in for two songs on the Supernatural set. The most fascinating thing for Bullfiddler was the strong bass lines the Texana Dames featured. He looked around the stage when the Dames began their set and noticed that the Dames did not have a bass player. Connie was playing strong bass lines on her piano for what turned out to be a very well received performance.

On that same gig Champ Hood played a set with Marvin Dykhaus and David Heath on his upright bass. Although Champ was at that time perhaps best known for his dynamic instrumental work on acoustic guitar and fiddle, he was also an accomplished songwriter and vocalist. Prior to the Auditorium Shores gig Champ had played on albums and on stage with everyone from Lyle Lovett to Jerry Jeff Walker. Champ had been writing and singing since his boyhood in South Carolina. The year before he played the ATCMHMR benefit he was named "Best Strings Player" by the 1993-4 Austin Chronicle Music Poll.

Opening for the Texana Dames, Champ and Ponty was a little known band, Poor Yorick. The band featured the son of the professional baseball pitcher who threw Willie Mays' his 500th home run. Yorick was a Vatican-educated bartender, a bug and bark-eating ex-boy scout who once marched in a Rose Bowl Parade. The band leader described his groups style as "rock, blue wave, western, yuppie rap, heavy aluminum, suburbanite soul and the like whose musical musings considered the sacred, the profane the profound and the insane". Bullfiddler could never forget Yorick or the rest of that summer lineup.

Mombo John Treanor added professional percussion to Leti's project. He was only 48 when he died at Seton Medical Center in Austin on August 10, 2001. Not only was he easy to work with in recording studios, Mombo was not afraid to discuss his illness. This made Bullfiddler uncomfortable; the last time they talked together was at a Central Market free gig Mombo spoke openly and unsolicited about his illness. He was playing percussion that night for Johnny Cash's old piano player Ernie Poole Ball who retired in Austin after his outstanding career with Cash and other Nashvillians.

Mombo became well known city-wide while playing drums for Beto y Los Fairlanes and energetic, exciting washboard with Marcia Ball. Bullfiddler met and came to know Mombo at The Continental Club where he was playing drums for Doak Short who opened every Tuesday night for Toni Prices 'Happy hippy Hour'. John would play only one song on washboard on Toni's set. Austinites remember John as a part of The Resentments with Scrappy Jud Newcombe and Jon Dee Graham. The Resentments played weekly for years at the Saxon Pub. In the studio Mombo John would hear a cut, comment on it with his unique form of percussion and send the enhanced tune back to the mixing board with a wide smile. Mombo was a talented stylist who lived his life fully, always playing his music with gusto. Mombo wrote and self-published a book of prison essays "The Power of Love and the Life of Dead Animals" while serving two years in El Reno, a federal penitentiary in Oklahoma for growing too much marijuana. Mombo never did not have a prison look or a jailhouse attitude. Mombo John played his final set at the Saxon Pub with one arm in a sling, with his wonderful smile and his characteristic great attitude.

Mombo was a musical student at UT with an interest in jazz that led him early on to Beto Skiles and the formation of Beto y los Fairlanes. The band became Liberty Lunch's first 'house band'. Mombo later had an adventure playing with Kris Kristofferson on a Kristofferson world tour. Anyone who jammed with John will forever remember his individualistic style of drumming, his energy and the way he made music richer sounding and more enjoyable. A memorial for Mombo was held at Threadgills North which Bullfiddler attended.

Even though Bullfiddler had positive recording sessions with Spencer Perskin he did not like having him for a roommate. Spencer is a true 'old school' rocker and when Bullfiddler rented a room to him and his wife his telephone would start ringing around ten in the evening and would ring off and on until dawn. Bullfiddler was working 60 hours a week during that period and he could only put up with that telephone ringing for month or so. Spencer would tell stories about his being in a Texas prison band with David Crosby during breaks while playing a hard fiddle both Shiva's Headband and for studio sessions with Whitey Ray Huitt, Leti de la Vega and many others.

Spencers long time day job was as a live model for the UT Art department. Spencer was interviewed by John Kelso while living at Bullfiddler's house. He referred to the house as a compound but Kelso referred to it as more of a complex.

Spencer not only told of playing with David Crosby of Crosby Stills and Nash at the Wynne unit of the Texas prison system in Huntsville, but also of the time his band opened for a band called Moby Grape and that a member of Moby Grape stole his bass amplifier. Spencer has, according to his own account put in more than 30,000 hours of nude modeling for art students at not only UT, but also the University of North Texas and Texas Woman's University.

Chapter 22

THE BLACK CAT

Paul Sessums owned and ran the smoke filled Black Cat Lounge on 6th Street and had another building with a stage and a back yard on Red River. It was at this deserted Red River club that Leti and Bullfiddler played their first live public gig with Calvin Russell opening, playing solo on the stage that chilly winter night. Leti and Bullfiddler didn't get paid anything other than the opportunity to play their bilingual music in front of an audience. Paul was outspoken, loved by all and passed away at an early age of 57 while driving back to Austin from Palacios. Paul had become interested in turning Palacios, an old near deserted gulf coast fishing town into an artist colony.

Paul protested the gentrification of 6th Street and did not participate in the Austin Chronicles South by Southwest Music Festival because he believed it was too commercial. He organized the 'South by So What' Festival and Bullfiddler had the pleasure of performing often during the simultaneous SXSW events. Paul always wore all-black with a black beret and he drove a black BMW motorcycle, rebelling against the Harley crowd. "Driveshafts are much smoother to ride long distances than belt or chain drives", Paul said when discussing his choice of motorcycles.

A sign in the first Black Cat, a thin bar 40 feet long and twenty feet wide on 6th Street said "The Black Cat is a smoking, beer drinking live original music club". The Black Cat opened in 1985, two years after Bullfiddler came to Austin. Paul's bar helped launch Ian Moore and groups like Two Hoots and a Hollar. The bar gave all of the door proceeds to the bands who were required to play three-hour sets with no breaks. Bullfiddler's neighbor Michael Condon and the Flametrick Subs got their start at the second Black Cat, becoming very popular with the young college crowd. After Paul's untimely death his wife Roberta and his daughter Sasha ran the second Black Cat until it caught fire and burned to the ground and never reopened, but Bullfiddler will always remember playing the first Black Cat one night with Jessie Taylor and those informal sets at Paul's non-club on Red River.

Chapter 23

INTERVIEWING WILLIE

On December 1st, 1993 Bullfiddler found himself working as the editor of the Garfield Tower, a small area paper that came out twice a month and circulated at all points east from Del Valle to Bastrop. The Garfield Tower publisher encouraged Bullfiddler to deliver the newspaper driving the publishers a white new Cadillac with an excellent sound system. Twice a month Bullfiddler toured the back roads to Bastrop, Elgin, Smithville, Lockhart and other fine Texas points of interest while listening to the Cadillacs loud radio.

One afternoon while driving down 71 from Austin to Garfield Bullfiddler spied Willie Nelson's bus and a film crew at one of the rest stops on the highway. When Bullfiddler snapped as to who was at that roadside park he told his publisher that he was going to go 'interview Willie'. The publisher gave Bullfiddler his blessing. On the way to the rest area Bullfiddler stopped at a local Garfield store and when one of the store clerks, a nineteen year-old girl found out where Bullfiddler was going asked Bullfiddler to let her tag along. Together they headed to the rest area amid thousands of bluebonnets and after parking he had to show the films security people his DPS Press Identification card. Soon out of the multicolored clean bus popped a calm Willie Nelson.

Willie Nelson was revisiting Highway 71 during the filming of "Songwriter' with Kris Kristofferson and Leslie Ann Warren. He and his film crew were filming road scenes at the camping area between Garfield and Del Valle when the very relaxed Nelson gave the Garfield Tower an interview. Willie was wearing a tee-shirt that said:

> Eiicy ose
> Polar Opp.

When folded up a particular way the nonsense on the tee shirt said something the Garfield Tower could not print.

Nelson talked about his old friend in Bastrop, Calvin Hunnycutt. Seems Nelson and Hunnyucutt go back some 30 years and that Calvin is also friends with the likes of Ray Price and Bob Wills.

"This is just one days shooting," Nelson said. "We're shooting travel scenes and filming a scene inside the bands bus. The bus scene takes place while we are on the roll."

David McGriffert, the assistant director of "Songwriter" added that one of the reasons Highway 71 is being used is because: "I got to know the area real well during the filming of "Honeysuckle Rose, and Willie has traveled this road often in the past." Nelson added that the shooting should be finished during the first week in January.

"I've wanted to do this movie for a long time," Nelson said. "Kris and I wrote the whole thing ourselves."

Willie then became a comedian. He told about how after a concert one of his roadies made love to a girl late one evening. Later the girl asked the roadie if he had Aides.

"Sure don't, honey," the roadie said.

"That's good", said the girl. "I sure don't want to catch that crap again".

Willie then related a story about a young American soldier stationed in the Pacific at the end or WWII. The soldier told his sergeant that he wanted to be a hero. The sergeant looked down at the boy and told him to go out near the front lines, stand up and yell that Hirohito is a son of a bitch. When an enemy pops his head up, shoot him and bring him back to camp.

A couple of hours later the GI all bruised and mangled came walking back into the camp and the sargent asked him what has happened.

"I did like you said," the soldier said, "I yelled out that Hirohito is a son of a bitch. A Jap stood up and yelled that Harry Truman was a son of a bitch. We were talking in the road to each other when we got hit by a truck".

Willie went on to define 'perfect pitch' which happens when you toss a banjo in a dumpster and it hits an accordion. Willie tried to learn how to play fiddle but he couldn't stand listening to himself, unlike Merle Haggard who after intensively practicing fiddle for six months on his band bus between shows was able to play fiddle before the thousands he regularly entertained while on the road. "Comes down to plain ol' desire," Willie said as he ended the interview to the music of Ray Price and the smell of marijuana coming from his bus.

After the interview with Willie Bullfiddler was ready to go back to his office but he now had a small female problem. Kris Kristofferson walked out of another bus and was standing near the door with his shirt off. The young girl Bullfiddler was with pointed to Kris and strongly suggested Kris be interviewed.

"I'm in a hurry," Bullfiddler told her, "gotta go."
"But he's right there!", she said. It sounded like she was pleading.
"Gotta deadline, gotta go now," Bullfiddler said.

Together they climbed into the car and the downcast store clerk never talked to Bullfiddler again after that episode. She idolized Kris and did not realize Bullfiddlers copy was due at the printers that evening. Ironically, Willie's mother died during the making of that picture and for the first and only time in Bullfiddlers journalistic career he had to 'stop the presses' so he could include condolences to Willie and his family in the Garfield Tower. The Garfield Tower adventure and Bullfiddlers working at a Willie picnic were the two times Bullfiddler met Willie Nelson. On both occasions Bullfiddler noted that there is nothing pretentious about Willie Nelson. What you see is what you get.

Chapter 24

SURVIVORS

Bullfiddler once walked Walter Hyatt to his car at Threadgills North after Walter played a short set with Champ Hood and Marvin Dykhaus. Bullfiddler had learned one of Walter's songs, 'As the Crow Flies' and he thanked Walter for writing that song. Walter died a horrible death later in a Value Jet crash in the swamps of Florida. Bullfiddler was sadly beginning to notice that some of the best, kindest and talented Austin musicians and songwriters were now passing away at a young age and Bullfiddler was finding himself attending funerals and memorials more and more often as he grew older. Bullfiddler consoled himself with the knowledge that there were many more survivors, hundreds of them. The Saxon Pub on South Lamar was home to Rusty Wier who, Bullfiddler thought was the friendliest entertainer in Austin and a good singer with a large vocal range to boot. With a cajun flavor on some of his songs and upbeat toe tappin' rhythm Rusty added unique warm sense of humor which seemed natural. Rusty also drank tequila while performing. He had written a song called "Chasing Quervo Gold' and when a barmaid delivered a shot of tequila to the stage Rusty told funny stories, giving people in the Saxon time to buy their own shot. Then Rusty recited a humorous toast and gulped the shot straight down as did the Saxon Pub's full house. Whenever Bullfiddler saw Rusty at the Saxon Pub, he drank shots with Rusty, along with up to 200 excited, friendly people. There were few strangers at the Saxon Pub by the time the bar closed after any of Rusty's gigs.

The Saxon Pub's PA system and the soundman that ran it in the 1990's were excellent in ability and quality with a good monitor system and decent stage sound. The exact opposite could be said of Steamboat Springs on Sixth Street which had one of the worst of Austins hundreds of club PA systems. Bullfiddler experienced both one weekend after being hired by Allen Dale to play two shows in one weekend, the first at the Saxon Pub and the second at the Steamboat. The duo did their set at the Saxon with no flaws technically or musically. The next night the two played their identical set at the Steamboat with constant feedback. The monitors did not work well, going off and on during songs and the stage volume was very trebly and not very loud making it hard for Bullfiddler to hear either Allen's vocals or guitar. Consequently on some songs Bullfiddler was out of sync, even starting a song in the wrong key. Both gigs were performed with one short twenty minute rehearsal at Bullfiddlers house. Allen worked as an Austin cab driver so together the duo rode to and from both gigs in a cab.

Another gimmick that was common at the Steamboat was the way they paid the bands. A few days before the gig the Steamboat would give the scheduled artist a handful of tickets good for a complimentary admission to the Steamboat. The tickets had the entertainers name and date of gig on them. It was up to the musician to give out these tickets to friends and at the end of the gig the performer and his band were given a dollar for every ticket collected at the door. Allen Dale and Bullfiddler gave out all their tickets and the Steamboat paid them seven dollars, giving Bullfiddler three dollars and fifty cents. He also had to pay his bar tab. The whole setup at the Steamboat was vastly different than that at the Saxon Pub where the bar bought drinks for the musicians. Later Bullfiddler played his bullfiddle during a video shoot at the Steamboat with Tony and the Tigers rockabilly band. The quality of both sound and video was so lousy that after a band viewing Tony took the only copy of the tape and "threw the video away", he said. He told Bullfiddler he burned it, Tony's wife Rosa confirmed the burning. Neither James Merideth or Bullfiddler received a copy of the one video Bullfiddler was involved in that was never shown on Austin Access television. Had the Steamboat hired pickers like Rusty Wier, Omar and the Howlers or the Resentments and played fair, the club might still be in business and competing with the beloved Saxon Pub.

Chapter 25

KERRVILLE KERVERT

On an evening in October, 1998 Bullfiddler talked to Rod Kennedy, owner-operator of the Kerrville Folk Festival about Rod's book 'Music from the Heart', a fifty-year chronicle of Rods life in music. Rod was having several book release parties and he hired Bullfiddler not to play music but to provide a PA system for a book release party at the Rock and Roll Emporium, a music store on 7th and Congress. Bullfiddlers fee would be forty dollars and a free signed copy of Rod's book. Rod already had the music lined up for the crowded event.

The book release party went off without a hitch. Rod had the use of a good sound system and Bullfiddler had a signed copy of what has come to be one of the most informative books on the music scene not only of Kerrville but in Austin as well. The book covers all of numerous other musical events from classical to folk and rock that Rod helped bring to Austin prior to the Folk Festivals first appearance in 1972. Rod was organizing music festivals in Zilker park in 1964 with the likes of Tom Paxton, Steve Fromholz and the Dallas County Jug Band. By the time Rod opened his first Kerrville festival he was an old hand at sponsoring musical events.

Late that evening when the book release party was over Bullfiddler gave Rod a copy of a CD a friend had recently recorded. Bullfiddler asked Rod if he would listen to the CD and see if Bullfiddlers friend could perform at a Kerrville Folk Festival. Rod took the CD and called Bullfiddler at home the next morning to say that he felt the vocals were not up to the standards of the festival and that there would be no spots available for Bullfiddlers friend. Since Bullfiddler did not tell his friend that he had submitted the CD to Rod in the first place, he did not relay the news of the rejection. A number of people who played on that CD were regulars at the Kerrville Folk Festival.

Bullfiddler had been told on many occasions to take his bullfiddle and campout at the festival. If he did, they said, he could find a lot of acoustic musicians to play along with at the evening campfires in the woods surrounding the ranch. Bullfiddler drove a motorcycle without a bass to Kerrville once, stayed for two hours, relished in the strong odor of burning ceder, did not see anyone he knew, drove back to Austin and has not visited Kerrville since. During Kerrvilles heyday Bullfiddler was playing weekly with local Austin groups and working day jobs and whenever Bullfiddler had vacation time it was never in May, when the Folk Festival is usually scheduled. During the annual festivals however there was always an influx of entertainment around Austin with Kerrvert musicians making a few extra bucks to help pay their expenses and hawk their recordings.

Rod's book, 'Music from the Heart' is very comprehensive with photos dating from the first Folk Festival in 1972. His photos show a number of popular Austin musicians in their youth and in their prime. There was going around a story about Rod Kennedy and God that caught Bullfiddlers attention. It seems that early on Rod while looking for some land outside of Kerrville and sat on a log to rest and take in the view of the Kerrville countryside.

"Rod," a voice boomed from the heavens, "this is God speaking. How are you?" God asked.

"I'm OK," Rod said, apparently not surprised about who he was talking with.

"Whassa matta?" God asked.

"Nothin' really, just tired I guess," Rod said.

"What would make you happy?" God asked Rod.

"Well, Nancylee and I have been looking for some land. Ideally we want to find a small ranch with a creek, and a natural amphitheater. I like music," Rod said.

It came to pass that Rod and Nancylee bought the site of the Kerrville Folk Festival. For years everything was running well, despite the rain. One evening after another exhausting festival Rod was sitting on the side of the main stage under an awning. God again spoke to Rod:

"Hi, Rod. Howya' doin'?" God asked.

"Oh, hey, Lord, I'm good. How are you doin'?" Rod replied.

"Do you have everything you need?" God asked.

"Yes, I do. Thanks Lord. I have the ranch, a host of fine talented musical friends and a Folk Festival we have out here annually. I have everything I could ever want. If there is anything I can do for you, Lord, just lemme know," Rod said.

"Come to think of it," God said," I could sure use a cold Budweiser longneck right about now."

"Sure thing," Rod said, "that'll be two-fifty."

A friend of Bullfiddlers, bassoon player Dianne Fry Cortez also wrote a wonderful book on her Kerrville experiences. Diane's book 'Hot Jams and Cold Showers' is a treasure of memories of local and nationally known musicians that have been in and around Austin for years. Diane's book is not only an account of her adventures as an bassoon player at the Kerrville Folk Festival, but it is also a love story about how she met and eventually fell in love with her husband, Javier. Her book captures the tastes and smells of Kerrville and records the good humor of a group of people with shared Kerrville experiences that are bonded together for life. The same can be said for the Austin music scene. If a musician hangs out in a barbershop long enough, he is gonna get a gig.

Chapter 26

THE MARRYING KIND

In the mid 1980'S there was a very unique music venue on Riverside drive called Thundercloud Subs Beergarden. Inside this 'garden' were two wood burning stoves, one next to the stage for the musicians and one at the back of the bar for the ping pong players. The smell of oak logs burning in the stoves and piled high outside was in the winter air but open windows helped keep the room well ventilated. An open mic was held there on Thursdays hosted by a unique, very humble songwriter, Rick Lane. Bullfiddler played a few gigs with Rick including a memorable one at Trophies on South Congress. On that night the musicians began to play and the night manager of Trophies approached the stage and told them they were too loud, asking the band to turn their music volume down. The band began to play another song and the irate manager again complained about the volume.

"OK. We quit," Rick Lane said quietly as he began to wrap up his guitar chord.

"Now, hold on," the manager said. "All ya gotta do is turn down some," he said apologetically.

"We quit," said Rick.

Rick had his school bus parked behind Trophies, so Bullfiddler and the musicians loaded up their gear into the old school bus, and together with most of the audience drove over to Ricks house on South Second street. There the musicians played in Ricks music room and partied by the campfire in the back yard until sunup.

Rick is a quality songwriter and gracious to a fault. During the open mic at Thundercloud Subs Rick rarely played any of his own well-crafted original songs but one night Bullfiddler showed up early and heard Rick perform six or seven of his songs to an empty house. Rick Lane has a good voice and a good way with words and wrote one song that Bullfiddler remembers well, 'Hitler's Daughter', a humorous song about an X.

On one occasion, after hearing Bullfiddler brag about the ministerial credentials he received from a church in Chula Vista California via Rolling Stone Magazine, Rick announced he and his girl friend Shelly were going to get married and asked Bullfiddler to perform the ceremony. Bullfiddler told Rick he would let him know if he could legally do such a thing and later that afternoon Bullfiddler called the Texas Attorney General's office and told one of the generals aids that he had obtained his ministerial credentials through the religion section of the classified ads in Rolling Stone Magazine and had not attended any kind of divinity or ministerial school. Could the Bullfiddler legally marry people in Texas. The Attorney General's representative said he would call Bullfiddler back, and within an hour returned the call and told Bullfiddler he could legally marry consenting adults as well as bury and baptize. Bullfiddler told Rick he could legally perform the ceremony and soon Rick and Shelly were married before literally hundreds of their friends on the Green Mesquites outdoor Barton Springs road stage accompanied by the smell of barbecue and the sight and aromas of thousands of flowers.

Bullfiddler wrote a wedding ceremony that was short with a prayer of the Apaches and a short item from Kahlil Gibran's 'The Prophet'. The wedding was complete with a band, flower girls, free food and free beer. Many of the women cried during the ceremony and Bullfiddler jokingly confided in Rick that he should have gotten into the religion business instead of music if only he had known he could get those reactions from the girls. The event reminded Bullfiddler of an ex-tent preacher he met while in graduate school in El Paso. The graduate student told some interesting tales about his adventures as a southern tent preacher. The preacher sold one of his short stories to Playboy magazine, describing southern attitudes about God, money and lust while he was still in graduate school.

In Austin word got around about Ricks great big wedding and for the next four or five years Bullfiddler married many couples, including couples he worked with at Austin Travis County Mental Health and Mental Retardation.

Chapter 27

DIAMOND SIMON

On cold winter nights at Rick Lanes open mic at Thundercloud Subs the musicians gathered around one of two wood burning stoves. Bullfiddler was scheduled to play one evening in 1986 but on that cold blustery night when Bullfiddler and friends took the stage the drummer began complaining that he couldn't play because the snare drum drumhead was slit open diagonally.

The musicians decided to call off their performance when a tall lanky guy with a thick friendly English accent stepped up and asked if he could play drums on that set. The guys in the band gave their OK and Diamond Simon from Sussex, England sat behind the drum kit, took the torn snare drum and moved it out of the way, took the floor tom and placed it where the snare would normally sit between the drummers knees. The musicians then rocked the room. Simon is no Gene Kruppa but he held his own, and Bullfiddler was impressed with Simon's clever ability The Bullfiddler and Simon later formed a band called 'The Go Cats' and were one of the last bands to play at The Austin Outhouse the night the bar closed. That band 'The Go Cats' consisted of Eddie Painter on percussion, Jeff Quellar on fiddle, Joe Phillips on percussion and Steve Manning on sax and Bullfiddler on his electric Fender bass. Herman the German and Das Cowboys was on that last Outhouse bill with a number of other bands, some soon forgotten.

'The Go Cats' also played a date at Threadgill's in North Austin and did something that was not done much at the venue. The band had a tenor sax instrumental in a song and they knew that Threadgills never had horns preferring acoustic guitars, fiddles, basses and mandolins. Steve Manning played his sax from a corner table rather than joining the band on stage and the 'Go Cats' blew the audience away with that stunt. As Simon and Bullfiddler became working co-musicians Bullfiddler went back to playing his electric bass on Simon's choice of rhythm and blues covers. Bullfiddler played R&B in Simon's band but it was not very fulfilling. He was developing a preference for original material.

On three occasions bands Bullfiddler played with were cross-booked in the same venue with another band. The first time a cross booking happened was at the Green Mesquite BBQ on Barton Springs road while playing bullfiddle with BNL Revue. Also booked that night was Ray Wilie Hubbard, a very popular Austin singer songwriter. BNL Revue was politely rebooked with no hard feelings and played the Green Mesquite often. The next two cross-bookings happened with Diamond Simon and the Roughcuts. They were to play on a Friday night at Charlie's Attic on Airport boulevard. When the band climbed the metal stairs to the second floor club they found a band already setting up on the stage. Simon asked the owner Charile, a former Marine about the situation. Simon pointed out that his band was booked, advertised in the papers and was listed on the marquis outside. "Talk to the band," was all Charlie would tell Simon. The fiddler in that band was a co-worker of Bullfiddlers at ATCMHMR and rather than get into an argument Simon called off the gig.

The next time Bullfiddler had a cross-booking was during the fall of 2003 at a club called Momo's on Austin's sixth street. The club had fired the guy that did the booking and the agent did not inform the club of the bookings he scheduled. Once again the drummer in that other band was someone Bullfiddler met while in Alcoholics Anonymous. Simon told the guys in the Roughcuts the night was canceled and Simon and Bullfiddler went to the Victory Bar and Grill in East Austin and auditioned acoustically for a gig. The manager was the lovely Eva who booked Simon and his band for a Saturday night gig the following month. The Roughcuts enthusiastically shared that bill with some of the Victory Grill regular eastside old-time Austin bluesmen.

Diamond Simon and The Roughcuts went on to perform in a number of venues in and around Austin. Simon always liked a loud horn section and the Roughcuts always played with a trio of horns consisting of a trumpet, trombone and tenor sax. That kind of musical power left Bullfiddler drained and exhausted after every gig. Having seen James Brown live in El Paso the Bullfiddler could close his eyes while playing through the Roughcuts version of James Brown's "I Feel Good" and imagine playing with Brown's band 'The Flames'. In fact, Roughcuts trumpet player Robert Ortiz did play one show with James Brown years earlier. Simon mastered the new technology of recording on a computer instead of tape and recorded an album of 'Diamond Simon and The Roughcuts' in 2004 and later a three song CD for Big Thomas Alexander. It was Big Thomas who regularly had the all-white Roughcuts play for his annual Juneteenth celebration marking the freedom of Black Americans. The Roughcuts played these Juneteenth gigs to a mostly all black audience.

The new computer recording technology is accurately featured on Paul McCartney's videos 'Chaos and Creation'. In it's process if done right the recording sessions are professional, clean and stress free. The Roughcuts recorded their projects in Simon's living room with Simon's obsessive attention to detail and sound mix quality one would normally find in an expensive professional recording studio. Simon with his knowledge of modern recording technology and musical direction made Bullfiddler sound like a real bass player, much to Bullfiddlers delight.

The Bullfiddler dropped out of The Roughcuts twice, once when he became involved in the bilingual project with Leti De La Vega and later after Bullfiddler entered an alcohol recovery program. During his second Roughcuts stint the Roughcuts again played at the Victory Bar and Grill where almost all the nationally well-known black blues and rhythm and blues artists played since the Victory's opening in 1946. The Roughcuts didn't make money on that dates but it was an honor to play on the same stage where WC Clark and other well known Austin musicians got their start. WC Clark as a teenager washed dishes at the Victory and was taught the basics by a number of qualified teachers that passed through the Victory Bar and Grill.

A memorable time Bullfiddler had performing with 'The Roughcuts' was at a gig with some of the Rolling Stones in attendance in 2007. At that time Simon was working with a great trumpet player, Robert 'Quarter Moon' Ortiz. Robert booked The Roughcuts to open for a friend of his, Jessie Botello at the Nuevo Leon Restaurant on Austin's East 6th street. On that Saturday night Botello had Bobby Keys playing sax on Botellos last four original songs. Bobby Keys had hooked up with the Rolling Stones in San Antonio in the late 1960's and has been playing and recording with them ever since. The Stones were scheduled to play at Austin's Auditorium Shores the following Sunday night.

The Roughcuts played their opening set on Nuevo Leon's large outdoor patio. The night was warm with a clear view from the stage and outdoor patio of Austin's overgrowing modern skyline. Bullfiddler ate enchiladas with flour tortillas. The chili was spicy hot and made him sweat. Tears filled his stinging eyes when he rubbed them without knowing he had chili residue on his hand. The Roughcuts only played seven songs and Bullfiddler was pumped when the set was over. His gear was backstage and the other band quickly set up. Botello's band began to play and Robert played trumpet with the band as did one of Joe Ely's guitar players. Bobby Keys came on stage to play on the last four songs and while in the middle of the first song Mick Jagger and Ron Wood walked in and sat at a table. One of the security guys pointed Mick and Ron out to Bullfiddler and his date and together they watched the two Stones more than they watched the band. Neither Stone had anything to eat or drink and Mick was smoking a long thin cigarette. After the last song the two Stones stood up and calmly walked out of the restaurant without much fanfare. As Mick and Ron passed before Bullfiddler and his friend Mick dropped the flame from his cigarette on the ground before entering the indoor part of the Nuevo Leon restaurant. Bullfiddler told his friend that she could get some of Mick's DNA if she wanted to retrieve the cigarette butt. She was closely watching them also and told Bullfiddler she saw Mick palm the unlit cigarette, leaving only the smoldering ash on the concrete steps. Bobby Keys and the band were great that Saturday night and the Stones played a never-to-be-forgotten Austin concert at Auditorium Shores the following Sunday.

Chapter 28

REHAB AND RECOVERY

On October 29, 1997 Bullfiddler paid off the mortgage on his Wallar creekside home, tied on a drunk at the Continental Club and was arrested by a woman APD officer on what turned out to be her first DWI bust. His emotions went wild that day as they ran the gauntlet from an extreme feel good high to the deepest of lows and fears while sitting in Travis County's new jail, de je vous of El Paso, only cleaner. Bullfiddler was arraigned before Judge Wilfred Aguilar in the Travis County Courthouse, made a personal recognizance bond and took the bus home by two that next afternoon, anxious to shower off that unique smell of jail. He paid for and picked up his car from Southside Wreaker that evening. One of the requirements of the PR bond was that the bondee had to attend AA meetings, a Victims Impact Awareness Panel and various county sponsored drug and drink schools.

On October 31, 1997, Bullfiddler attended his first meeting of Alcoholics Anonymous in Travis County at a little North Austin recovery club. At that time the club was across the street from the Yellow Rose, a topless club Austin institution and the Centennial Liquor Store, both on Lamar street in north central Austin. The room where the meetings were held had no windows, looked and smelled freshly painted, black, with no ventilation. Bullfiddler sat in a folding metal chair and listened as the group recited the Serenity Prayer. He went to the evening meeting with a plan to leave at 8:45 pm so he could stop by the Centennial Liquor store on his way home. Bullfiddler planned to buy a half pint of tequila but he became so wrapped up in what the speaker at that meeting was talking about, something about AA being "the last house on the block" that he stayed for the entire meeting. Bullfiddler ended up holding hands with people he would have had a hard time seeing himself associated with and together the group said the Lord's Prayer and the often quoted saying: "Keep coming back, it works if you work it".

Bullfiddler kept coming back to that blue collar working man's AA club for three weeks, trying what his sponsor suggested, make 90 meetings in 90 days and then on that sponsors advice went out AA 'club hopping'. By this time Bullfiddler was convinced of two important things: he had a lot to lose if he kept drinking and that there needed to be a major change in his lifestyle if he wanted to improve the quality and dignity of his life. He had better 'take the cotton out of his ears and put it in his mouth', as the saying goes or in other words shut up and pay attention at meetings. Bullfiddler began to learn how to listen. Austin had over thirty different AA groups throughout Travis County, so there were plenty of clubs, each with their own personality to choose from and Bullfiddler attended for a while a small group in north Austin. He took his sponsors advice and went to 90 meetings in 90 days and realized that he was not an alcoholic. To Bullfiddler an alcoholic is one who cannot have just one or two drinks. When Bullfiddler quit smoking cigarettes, smoking just one cigarette caused him to return to a full-blown cigarette smokers habit. That addictive cigarette behavior is the same with alcohol for alcoholics. Bullfiddler could always take just one or two drinks and leave without having to drink to oblivion but once he smoked one cigarette he always bought a pack shortly after smoking that cigarette. Quitting smoking had to be an all or nothing proposition with no half measures. Sometimes though, Bullfiddler did get a little loud and stupid when he over drank, and on reflection while working AA's 12 Steps he realized that he had made some bad decisions while drunk. He also began to realize that he relied on alcohol for courage.

"You wanna dance?", "sure, lemme have a shot or two first."

On meeting new musicians booze or pot was an ice breaker. The same thing applied to interpersonal relationships. He realized that alcohol broke down self imposed barriers and that now that he was 50 years old he had to develop the fortitude to be able to socialize and play music without crutches, and this did not come easy for Bullfiddler.

By 1997 there were obvious signs that Bullfiddlers drinking behavior was becoming a problem although the problem existed for years prior to Bullfiddlers awareness of it. He had been asked to leave clubs and some of his friends homes. Eddie Wilson, the owner of Threadgill's personally asked Bullfiddler to leave Threadgill's North after Bullfiddler walked in to the music room all high. He was celebrating the release of his second CD with his friend Leti. He had been celebrating because they were very proud of their first CD and by the time the second one was bought out by Deep South Records Bullfiddler had been snorting speed and did so two or three times a month. Speed was all over Austin and very easy and cheap to obtain. He was also smoking pot daily and drinking tequila and beer whenever he was in a place where the combination was sold.

The more adventures and success Leti and Bullfiddler experienced the more Bullfiddler indulged in chemicals that would alter his mind and his behavior.

On the day the two were given a box of their latest CD, the two went out and ate liver and onions with mashed potatoes and cream gravy and Threadgills spicy cornbread with real butter. The two then had a drink and walked home. After returning home Bullfiddler did a line of crank, walked back to Threadgill's and ordered a shot of tequila. Eddie Wilson approached Bullfiddler, looked straight into the Bullfiddlers glazed-red eyeballs not-at-home look and politely yet firmly asked Bullfiddler to leave his restaurant.

The Bullfiddler put up no argument and left, thanking his lucky stars. Eddie was such a gentleman about it all and he is stout as a bull and could easily have thrown Bullfiddler out on his ear with little effort. Eddie has since let Bullfiddler back in to his two his two music clubs, Threadgill's North and Central but that incident was an example of the kind of things that caused Bullfiddler to take 'recovery' seriously. Bullfiddler quit drinking, and using speed within two days of his arrest and in so doing also had to get away from old friends and old playgrounds. Bullfiddler quit playing music out of the house for over two years, trying to get used to living without mind and mood altering substances.

Bullfiddler regularly attended his first AA club which had since moved to the other side of North Lamar. There was a huge table in front of a large plate glass window in the club lobby where Bullfiddler and others in recovery would spend hours between meetings playing dominoes and watching the view out that picture window of what they laughingly called the 'crack channel', so named because the view was of a cheap motel across the street that housed hookers and dealers doing box office North Austin business. Together in the well ventilated room the group would watch it all including the occasional busts by the police who often were called to the club itself to subdue someone who was drunk and rowdy.

The white clean Chevy Blazer of Bullfiddlers was stolen from the front of that club one rainy night. Bullfiddler was talking with Bob W., and when he went outside he noticed his truck was gone. Bullfiddler recovered his truck the next day when Southside Wrecker in South Austin called to tell Bullfiddler where his wrecked truck was being stored. The thief had broken the door lock, the steering column and used a screwdriver to make two contacts to 'hot wire' the car. The Bullfiddler saw the damage and with the help of a Southside Wrecker learned how to hot wire his car with a screw driver. Bullfiddler again paid Southside Wrecker $145.00 and never did get that truck ignition or door lock repaired, thinking that he had been victimized twice, once by the thief and once by the wrecker service and that possibly his truck might get stolen again. Apparently the thief while driving off in Bullfiddlers stolen truck found Bullfiddlers wallet with sixty dollars cash and in the thief's excitement crashed the truck into a pylon in front of a nearby convenience store, in a hurry probably to buy some beer. There, thought the Bullfiddler was a thief who could not handle prosperity.

Bullfiddlers' only physical fight in Austin since arriving in 1982 occurred during his early recovery period. A scruffy very competent older fiddle and mandolin player, Willie the Fidd was crashing in a room in Bullfiddlers home and drank daily while Bullfiddler was in early sobriety. While playing a free show at the Austin State School the Willie the Fidd cussed up a streak on the microphone in front of an audience of mentally retarded people while playing a benefit for free at Neo's at the Austin State School. During their break a staff member approached Bullfiddler and asked him to speak with the fiddler about his obscene language. The staff member reminded Bullfiddler that the use of obscene language toward or around MHMR consumers could constitute consumer abuse, a criminal offense. Bullfiddler talked to Willie the Fidd about his language and the fiddler became verbally abusive toward the Bullfiddler.

"If they don't like my language they can go—themselves," the fiddler said.

"I will not play out with you anymore if you have been drinking." the Bullfiddler said.

"Go—yourself," said the fiddler.

When the two returned to Bullfiddlers house after the gig Bullfiddler made the mistake of taking a bottle of whiskey away from the fiddler. The two got into a shoving argument that turned into an all out fight. Bullfiddler had to call APD and together they both ended up in Austins' Brackenridge hospital; the fiddler had a broken arm and a broken collarbone while Bullfiddler had a sore testicle that later swelled to the embarrassing size of a softball. The Bullfiddler had surgery on that testicle and went to great lengths to avoid playing with the fiddler who over the years had taught the Bullfiddler basic bullfiddle techniques, mandolin, guitar, vintage bluegrass and country and western music. In his younger years the old fiddler played with Hank Thompson and the Brazos Valley Boys and with Charlie Pride. As a child the fiddler was the son of a doctor and his mother taught him all the basic guitar chords. Like his father, Willie the Fidd was a quick learner who also learned how to play bass, dobro, mandolin and fiddle with a smattering of accordion. His music was up tempo cajun and he was not a one key wonder. Willie the Fidd played music in every key and has been playing solo on Congress Avenue in downtown Austin for over thirty years. As a nine year old childhood prodigy Willie the Fidd had his own weekly musical radio show that ran for four years while growing up in Florida.

The old fiddler once saved Bullfiddler's life while Bullfiddler was living in a trailer at Shady Grove on Barton Springs road. One night over a campfire in 1986 Bullfiddler told Willie the Fidd that he felt suicidal whereupon the Fidd began telling funny stories and soon had Bullfiddler laughing so hard he tripped over the campfire. Bullfiddlers laughing began to physically hurt so he walked to Barton Springs for some relief. The next day Bullfiddlers ribs felt like they were broken and he has not thought about suicide since. That night Willie the Fidd told Bullfiddler over a hot roaring summer campfire of how he lost his interest in playing any instrument in a band, preferring to play solo on the streets. One of his secrets is that he has a long history as a competent well rounded studio session player.

Over the crackling of the burning oak logs the fiddler told Bullfiddler that all he needed was enough money for tobacco, a hamburger at Whataburger and a pint of whiskey. Occasionally after a good weekend on the streets he would get a room for one or two nights. He usually camped out in the secluded creek-fed forests of South Austin during the winter and spent the summers in Colorado, often pistol shooting at empty hanging whiskey bottles while drinking hard liquor and swapping stories with his journalist friend Hunter Thompson.

Honest recovery can lead to some very lonesome times in the beginning, especially if one is involved in the music scene. When one decides to quit using drink and drugs one also quits associating with both those who sell and those who share in the high times. In Austin you can not throw an enchilada without hitting a guitar player and the same was true with drug connections. In 2000 after Bullfiddler had been clean for over two years he was diagnosed with Hepatitis C. Hep-C is also known in Austin as the musicians disease because so many musicians have had it and some have died from it. One catches Hep-C mainly through sharing needles. Bullfiddler received a tattoo at Beverlies during one of his early gigs there. The Bandito was fresh out of Huntsville prison and was doing everything he could to earn enough scratch to buy a motorcycle. Bullfiddler had the figure of a bullfiddler tattooed on his back and suspects that this is where he contacted Hep-C since the disease cannot be transmitted through sexual contact or snorting drugs. The Bullfiddler thought the tattooist should have cleaned his needles.

When Bullfiddler quit buying and using drugs some people he thought were friends went off with those who did not have a problem with using drugs. Bullfiddler and Simon reunited to play a benefit for Alcoholics Anonymous. It seemed that after that night many in recovery in North Austin wanted to be his friend and were supportive of his desire to quit drinking. On occasion at recovery meetings some well known musicians would speak at the speakers meeting. They shall remain anonymous, in keeping with the program tradition but some of the recovering musicians want it known who they are in the hope they can influence others to get clean and stay clean. One of the recovering musicians, a former member of Stevie Ray Vaughan's Double Trouble told a crowded speaker meeting one night about what it was like to perform his first 'clean' gig before 30,000 people. Another successful Austin songwriter would related how the music business for him had changed when he cleaned up, becoming more respectable and profitable. He did admit that his 'hits' were written while he was loaded. To the programs credit there are numerous Austin musicians, blue collar workers, lawyers and doctors and judges who attend AA meetings and share their experiences, strengths and hopes with other people in recovery. They all hope they can influence at least one member of the audience to change and adopt sobriety as his new lifestyle.

Austin passed a no smoking ordinance after Bullfiddler entered recovery. All the live music club and cafe owners were worried that they would lose their patrons who had been smoking and drinking for years. Bullfiddler returned to the Roughcuts band and played the Poodle Dog Lounge with Diamond Simon in November, 2005 after Bullfiddler had been sober for a few years. The smoking law was in effect, but the way the law was written, if the bar did not leave out ashtrays, posted no smoking signs and asked patrons not to smoke, there were no other penalties. The Poodle Dog on Burnett road had smoking in the bar with patrons using old beer cans for ashtrays and keeping an eye out for guests who looked like undercover cops. Many compared the behavior to that of the speakeasy's during prohibition. It was during this period that Bullfiddler first quit smoking cigarettes only to later relapse once again after the death of his long-time dog. During one of the Roughcuts gigs at the Poodle Dog, Robert Ortiz musically hijacked the band creating a round of abandon and good humor.

Robert asked Bullfiddler if he knew any Freddie Fender (Baldemer Juerta) songs. Bullfiddler told Robert he knew them all, so with the drummer in agreement the three of them played through three or four Freddie Fender songs, catching the jealous Englishman by surprise. Simon did not know the tunes so he 'faked it' on his turned down Gibson guitar and the band received a spirited response as Simon regained control of his band. That evening it had been snowing and Robert fell on the curb while helping the band load their gear into the van in front of the bar. Robert needed no stitches but was sore for about a week and worried about what effect the accident would have on his superior trumpet playing abilities.

Throughout his years in Austin Bullfiddler played the Poodle Dog with one group or another. The bar does not have a stage so the band sets up on the floor, mixing directly with the patrons. When some of the biker girls got off work at the local topless bars around Austin, they would come into the Poodle Dog and dance to the R&B while checking themselves out in the mirrors that lined the Poodle Dog walls. Often the bands rhythm would be affected because the musicians would find themselves playing to the rhythm of the dancers instead of what was needed for the song. On occasion Bullfiddler changed up his bass pattern in the middle of a song to watch the dancers adapt their movements to his bass work.

When 9/11 happened Bullfiddler was disturbed as were all Americans. Some 'rednecks' in recovery at the time wanted to nuke the entire Persian Gulf region and turn the Islamic world into a sheet of glass, even though AA has a tradition that states that the program should "have no opinion on outside issues hence the AA name ought never be drawn into public controversy". For a religious group, a lot of the folks in recovery with Bullfiddler at that time had a hell of a resentment against anything Islamic. Having lived and worked in North Yemen Bullfiddler felt he understood some of the resentment the Islamic world has toward the west. Bullfiddler never would try to justify 9/11 but he needed more spirituality than what he was currently getting at his local blue collar AA.

Chapter 29

GETTING RELIGION

Bullfiddler had played a few acoustic gigs in the 1980's with Carol Simmons in a coffee house setting at the First Unitarian Universalist Church in central Austin. She later played piano in the '90's with Bullfiddler's Los Downbeats at Auditorium shores. Carol had years earlier released two 45 rpm records and was a regular performer at the Continental Club. After 9/11 Bullfiddler remembered those gigs and how it compared with the first coffee shop he attended in El Paso in the basement of a church at the foot of Mount Franklin. He also remembered Champ Hoods memorial at the Austin Unitarian Church and had recalled fond memories of playing the short sets at the Church with Carol. Bullfiddler decided to return to that church for services the weekend after 9/11, something he never would have done if he was still drinking and drugging.

What Bullfiddler heard from the pulpit and the vibes he felt that Sunday were good reasons Bullfiddler needed to start going to Sunday services on a regular basis. Besides the recent memory of the tear jerking Champ Hood memorial, there are a number of X-Peace Corps Volunteers in the congregation and the minister and the congregation seemed to tolerate varying lifestyles while trying to find good and positive aspects from all religions. No one at that church ever told Bullfiddler he was going to go to hell if he didn't fly right or believe a certain way just as nobody in Alcoholics Anonymous ever told him he was an alcoholic or who his higher power should be. The church spiritually had something in common with AA in that they both believed in a 'higher power of your choosing'.

Emerson and Thoreau were mentioned at the Unitarian Church often as were teachings from various religions and religious leaders ranging from Buddhism and Catholicism to Zen and Judaism with touches of Islam thrown in. The all-faiths openness of the Unitarian Church combined with the churches tolerance of differing peaceful lifestyles and a wide variety of 'heady' music was all Bullfiddler needed to begin putting down his spiritual roots and start developing a new way of life. The church led Bullfiddler to a new appreciation of nature and many new forms of Austin church music. The church music director, the young genius Brent Baldwin chose choral music ranging from Leonard Cohen, John Lennon, gospel to Bob Dylan occasionally inviting in guest artists from the Austin Symphony or other Austin church choirs. Shortly after joining the church Bullfiddler was recruited to play in a church combo The Dirgibles.

The spelling of The Dirgibles was a unique creation of Maryjane Fords Unitarian mind and was appropriate for the slower rhythm of the music they perform. The band did not perform Johnny Cash's 'Get Rhythm', until they met Bullfiddler who induced the musicians to back him up on a song attesting to the value of rhythm. However the 'band' did not have a drummer and for the first time in Bullfiddlers musical career he used a music stand as did the others in the band. The musicians did not have or use head charts. At his very first Dirgible rehearsal Bullfiddler was sitting on the piano bench when the bassoonist, Diane Fry Cortez began playing 'Faded Love', a country and western standard. Bullfiddler turned around and began playing along with Diane on the piano. It quickly dawned on Bullfiddler that he was doing a duet on a C&W tune with a bassoon player. Diane not only authored her book on her adventures at the Kerrville Folk Festival but also co-authored 'Tipi', a book about building and maintaining tipis. Like a new comer at an Alcoholics Anonymous meeting Bullfiddler kept quiet, played the bullfiddle the best he could and went with the flow.

The Dirgibles have since played a number of gigs at both Wildflower (a south Austin Unitarian Church) and First UU on Grover Avenue and with the Austin Quakers. The Dirgibles focused on old Americana music, such as the Carter family (pre-Johnny Cash) and old country and gospel standards. The piano player, Jim Barry occasionally introduces an old 1950's rock song during rehearsals. Jim is a George Jones fan with George Jones hats and memorabilia scattered around his living room. He shares Bullfiddlers interests in the historical histories of the Dirgibles music as well as the original well-crafted 'nature' songs that band leader Maryjane Ford has written.

For a CPA Maryjane is a wonderful songwriter who writes story songs with a heavy nature influence. Maryjane is very different in that she is content with the recognition she gets in the church and has no interest in performing out in 'public'. Trying to interest her in recording is a futile exercise because Maryjane has no interest in recording or selling any of her songs. Her calm peaceful attitude took Bullfiddler a while to get used to because up until he met Maryjane,the songwriters he knew focused on getting their material out to as many listeners players as possible.

During this new phase of Bullfiddlers music life in Austin he began once again to play some pick-up gigs as a duo with Diamond Simon sans Roughcuts. While in the bars and cafes Bullfiddler noticed everyone was not drinking alcohol like he thought they were, and were not as drunk as he thought when he was drinking. This is a common observation drinkers make when they stop drinking. By now the Bullfiddler was getting a solid musical fix from the Unitarian Church. Like Bullfiddler, Simon felt he had played enough of Wilson Pickett and James Brown to last a lifetime. Simon fired his Roughcuts, canceled gigs that he had booked through 2008, sold the Roughcuts web site to a diamond dealer in California and filed for divorce.

Simon and Bullfiddler played acoustically as a duo at a bar in Manor, Texas called The Oaks. At The Oaks Simon introduced Bullfiddler to Regan Marie Brown, a lovely songwriter with a uniquely appealing voice, a good sense of rhythm and an excellent command of the English language. Professionally she is a writer having written two books and at the time was popular on the acoustic Austin and Hill Country music scene. Regan Marie and the Bullfiddler had a short stint together, performing at Hill's, the Cactus Cafe, The Oaks in Manor, Texas, Sam's Town Point in Manchaca, Texas, BD Rovers, Old Ross', Giddy-Ups in Manchaca, Texas, Poodies out by Spicewood and a Friday night open mic at 290 West, formerly the Little Wheel. It was at the Little Wheel in 1986 that Bullfiddler was fired from his second band job with Richard Patureau and the Bayou Bandits where they also hosted an open mic for over a year. Bullfiddler and 290 West have a history, they know each other.

Regan and Bullfiddler were both born in El Paso, Texas in the same hospital, Southwestern General. Early in their friendship they compared birth certificates. Her mother was a journalist; Bullfiddlers mother wrote for the El Paso Times for 16 years. The two were amazed at the numerous coincidences and things the two had in common, both recalled working for cranky editors, felt the reward of a byline and know what it is like to have someone else cover one of their songs using great Austin musicians. However Bullfiddler began drinking and smoking cigarettes more often. He saw he was returning to some dangerous old behaviors so he retreated to the safety of the church.

Bullfiddler had the unfortunate opportunity to see a negative side of the music business in Austin. The first show Bullfiddlers friend Regan Marie played her music was at Old Ross's Cafe on North Lamar in Austin. The cafe was forced to shut down their acoustic open mic due to ASCAPs financial demands. ASCAP is a national organization that makes money for American composers and songwriters. The organization threatened fines and court action if Ross did not pay steep royalties so the cafe decided to quit having live music rather than fight an agency with heavy legal clout. Consequently, some good singer-songwriters who played there weekly are now playing elsewhere. The performers were paid with tips (there was no cover charge at the door) and dinner.

ASCAP has successfully closed down other live music venues in Austin. The ironic question here is that the musicians played original music as opposed to 'covers', so if no ASCAP writers material was performed, then one asks why were the venues assessed the penalty. All an ASCAP agent had to do was report hearing one 'cover' song. This ASCAP business combined with the non-smoking ordinance made live music venues challenging for musicians in comparison to the easy access musicians had in the 70's and 80's. Proportionately there are many live music bars in and around Austin that do hire bands, hold open mics and grudgingly pay annual ASCAP fees.

In Austin for years a street musician had to get a permit from the city to play on the streets during, say, 'The Pecan Street Festival', but every now and then a street musician like Jerry King gets 'discovered', recorded and turned into what some agents call 'product'. That kind of discovery happens a lot in Austin which helps explain the city's music mystique and excitement.

Chapter 30

TEXAS WICCANS AND QUAKERS

    Meanwhile back at the church, The Dirgibles had Maryjane Ford on guitar and 4-string banjo, Ed Slegle on violin and cello and Jim Berry on piano, Diane Fry Cortez on bassoon, Mark Skrabacz on harmonica and vocals and Bullfiddler on his 'illustrated' bullfiddle. This group did not use drugs, smoke a joint or even have a shot of tequila before a gig or a rehearsal but they have shared some French and Italian wine. The gigs at church are varied . . . the Wiccans meet at the church to celebrate nature and the changing of the seasons. Herman Nelson one of the elder songwriters at the Austin Unitarian Church asked Bullfiddler to play bass on a song Herman wrote years ago and was going to sing for a Wiccan gathering. At the first rehearsal Nelson played the song on his old acoustic guitar but decided during that rehearsal that the only instrumentation needed was the bullfiddle sound. At the Wiccan gig, many Wiccans were dressed in black and since the holiday was also a day of remembrance, one of the leaders recited a long list of people that died in 2007. Then Herman sang his song with a six person chorus and Bullfiddlers bullfiddlin' in the background.
    The Dirgibles played for the International Folk Dance Festival Annual bash. The music is basically about various aspects of nature. He began playing old Union and worker songs as well as old 'Peace' standards with the Austin Quakers, a super peace living warm group of people whose church is in the heart of East Austin and has close ties to the Unitarians. While camping out in the Quakers backyard Bullfiddler noticed the smells of roasting vegetables and huge trees completely surrounding the Quaker compound. All this and the crackling of dry leaves underfoot gave one the feeling of being in the peaceful countryside instead of in the heart of Austin.
    The Quaker gigs came about because of their ties to Maryjane and other Austin Unitarians who are 'simpatico' with the Quakers. The Quakers gave

the Unitarian church a campground near Kerrville and many Unitarians and their friends camp there during the Kerrville Folk Festival. The Quaker's once a month musical sessions are a far cry from the gigs Bullfiddler played in El Paso and Juarez. The Quakers are composed of hardcore peacenicks and their choice of music dates to the Weavers, Peter, Paul and Mary, the Kingston Trio as well as Woodie Guthrie, Pete Seeger and often took Bullfiddler back to the first coffee house he experienced in El Paso. Church music with Maryjane, music with the Quakers keeps Bullfiddler busy and more content artistically, especially now that money and rent is not an issue. The musicians Bullfiddler is not working with seem to understand the definition of empathy. Too often in his past Bullfiddler noted that some star wannabes were friendly to those who were interested in their projects but turned a deaf ear to their musicians when they offered song lyric or arrangement suggestions. Many bandleaders are fans of the Frank Sinatra and Elvis 'My Way' philosophy and often showed no interest in or gave support to their backup musicians own projects. Too often Bullfiddler met wannabes who were 'friends in deed', but he has fond memories of those talented musicians who would gladly support the lesser knowns and had tamed their egos.

Epilog

Austin has much to offer both professional and amateur musicians including Bullfiddler. Texans love fiddle players and bullfidders. Playing upright bass while sober and off drugs has not only improved Bullfiddlers bullfiddlin'. There are so many creative singer songwriters in Austin that finding people to play music with is the least of any musicians concerns. Rent however is much higher than it was when Bullfiddler first came to Austin in 1982. In 1982 a musician could afford to live cheaply in Austin. Bo 2000 one has to have a trust fund, a good job or like communal living to make it financially. In Austin in the '80's Stevie Ray Vaughn and Blaze Foley never paid any rent with cash. Fans would gladly give them room and board for free.

Austin is much quieter now than in 1982 because bands don't rehearse at full volume in apartments or homes, opting to rehearse in rehearsal halls or acoustically at home. In 1982 one was hard pressed to not hear music during an afternoon neighborhood walk but now Austin is very peaceful and relatively quiet considering the cities rapid population explosion.

Kinky Friedman began his Texas career as a bandleader. He ran for Governor in Texas in 2007 while Bullfiddler was playing playing church music. Kinky lost the election big time to Rick Perry. Bullfiddler thought it was much easier for a Jew to play music in Texas than to run for and win a statewide office. Bullfiddler never could get into Kinky and the Texas Jewboys music with such chauvinistic lyrics as 'keep your biscuits in the oven and your buns in bed'. He read most of Kinky's novels, but he really appreciated the work Kinky was doing to save homeless dogs. Bullfiddler had been rescuing dogs since his arrival in Austin, noting that the 'animal therapy' helped Bullfiddler keep his sanity and gladly accepted some personal responsibility, something that can be a challenge for any active musician. In fact, Bullfiddler's dogs have kept the thieves who often thrive on musical instruments at bay. While some of his neighbors experienced break ins, Bullfiddler noted that a doped up thief would not enter a home where there was a dog he did not know personally.

In the music world of Texas musicians can come full circle. A good example of this is the San Antonio band Krayola. One evening Bullfiddler was surfing MySpace and he found and listened to the music of Krayola. He e-mailed the band and one of the members wrote back saying he had a copy of a review Bullfiddler wrote of a Krayola performance in El Paso. The review appeared in The El Paso Times dated May 25, 1978. On the 23rd of 1978 Krayola had given a performance at El Paso's New Buffalo with an outstanding second set and two encores. The New Buffalo was located in downtown El Paso across from the Plaza Park was the same club Bullfiddler saw Asleep At The Wheel a short time later.

Krayola first set was rough due to technical problems. In fact, the concert started an hour late due to technical difficulties. On their second set they covered early Beatles with excellent vocal harmonies and ended their last set with Lucy in the Sky with Diamonds and A Hard Day's Night. The band also covered The Kinks, The Beach Boys the Searchers Tommy James and the Shondells, The Byrds, Buffalo Springfield and Jefferson Airplane, again with excellent vocal harmonies. What bombed with the audience was their campy Beach Boy take off called Surfin' Rio Grande. The group was highly professional, playing one song right after another with witty short patter between songs and sets. On their second set Bullfiddler noted that Krayola was dressed in Sgt. Pepper's costumes.

There was a small bone of contention that Krayola had with Bullfiddler and they mentioned it in an e-mail from Krayola. In his review, Krayola reminded Bullfiddler, the review mistakenly claimed that the bass player played with a pick while Paul McCartney use his fingers. Bullfiddler was wrong, Krayola noted and MySpace videos later proved it. Still, the band saved that review and discussed it with Bullfiddler some 30 years after its publication. Krayola has been playing music for thirty years! Bullfiddler was thirty when he wrote that review.

The 'Music Capitol of the World' now has other aspects about the town it did not have when Bullfiddler arrived in Austin in 1982. As a result of the NAFTA Treaty, hundreds of trucks have to slow down as they pass through Austin on the I-35 corridor to Mexico and hundreds of trucks leave the border daily heading north passing slowly through Austin on their way, producing heavy emissions and snarling traffic. The quality of the air changed almost over night when NAFTA took its full effect but it is still cleaner than that of El Paso. Every evening, all night long, 24-7 the I-35 freeway that runs through Austin to San Antonio is congested. However, now that gasoline is up to four dollars a gallon for regular, there is a lot less inner-city traffic. Students and other people are staying home and the roads in Austin except for rush hour are eerily calm. Traffic is much slower between rush hours, because the students can't afford to cruise, opting to go on line or watch television at home. The positive side of all this is that music is always more in demand during economic hard times and Austin has many freebie outdoor concerts.

Austin offers a musician numerous choices in style, classical, jazz, folk, hard rock, country, R&B, Latin and Conjunto and bluegrass. This diversity along with Austins' evergreen climate and warm winters keeps Bullfiddler from ever contemplating returning to El Paso. Bullfiddler has not made Austin's A-list but at 60 has survived in the wide world of Texas music with many fond memories of his musical adventures. The most exciting aspect of playing bullfiddle in Austin is not knowing what the musical future holds. There is a saying: 'a person needs three things to be happy . . . 'something to do, something to love and something to look forward to'. Your playing where? Recording when? With new live music venues opening regularly the possibilities and combinations of musical gigs, talented personalities and egos are un-imaginable, making waking up every morning the beginning of a new adventure, despite the smog, high rent and soaring gas prices.

The 'Live Music Capitol of the World' is where even an amateur acoustic musically illiterate bass player can become part of the thriving scene providing the musician can obtain gasoline. Throughout the 1980's and '90's gas was under a dollar a gallon. A number of Austin bands are now playing fewer and fewer out of town gigs because the price of gas eats up the poor wages most local bands receive from playing out of town venues. Band buses, often using diesel get notoriously poor gas mileage. As of May, 2008 diesel gasoline was selling for four dollars and fifty cents a gallon. Consequently a lot of bands are staying in Austin and are playing more and more local gigs, pleasing thousands of Austin music lovers with the wide variety.

A strong desire to play music, having the right musical environment and an economical ride is almost as good as having musical talent and being able to read music. There is no doubt that Bullfiddlers bass playing improved because he was in cahoots with and often competed against hundreds of other suburb players from all over the world. He often wondered what kind of a musician he would have become had he stayed in El Paso with the frontier towns limited regional musical exposure.

Index

A

Airport Blvd, 57
Alcoholics Anonymous, 107, 110, 117, 118
Alcoholics Anonymous., 114
Alfredo Leal, 35
Alices Restaurant, 78
America, 40
Ampeg amp, 59
Anapra, 37
Antones, 30, 64
Antones next door to Rubys BBQ, 65
APD, 74, 110, 113
Appa Perry, 78
Apple Records, 40
Ario Guthrie, 78
Armadillo, Beverlies, 56
ARRRIBA, 89
Art Lewis, 30
ASCAP, 119
Asleep at The Wheel, 51, 69
Asleep at the Wheel, 41, 42, 48
Asylum Street Spankers, 89
ATCMHMR, 65, 66, 68, 69, 71, 72, 73, 92, 107
Auditorium Shores, 66, 68, 73, 92, 108, 109
Austex, 56, 77, 78, 83
Austin Access TV, 81
Austin Chronicle, 56, 59, 69, 77, 90, 92, 94
Austin City Limits, 51, 70, 74

Austin Songwriters, 69
Austin State Hospital, 73, 86
Austin Symphony, 49
Austin Television, 60
Austin-Travis County Mental Health, 65

B

Baldemer Juerta, 115
Banda, 57
Bar Mitzvah, 15, 16
Barton Springs, 44, 66, 74, 105, 107
Bastrop, 46, 52, 57, 58, 96, 97
BD Rovers, 119
Beach Boys, 26, 35, 36
Beatle bass, 45
Beatles, 20, 26, 27, 28, 34, 40, 64
Beatles and Bob Dylan, 22
Bergstrom Airbase, 46
Bergstrom Airport, 45
Beto Skiles, 93
Beto y los Fairlanes, 93
Beverlies, 56
Big Thomas Alexander, 107
Biggs Air Base, 25
Billy Benton, 54
Black Cat, 78, 86, 94, 95
Blaze Foley, 54, 57, 74, 76, 81, 83, 123
BNL Revue, 61, 62, 63, 64, 65, 66, 78, 87, 88, 107

Bob Hernandez, 68
Bob Hope, 69
Bobby Fuller, 20, 29
Bobby Fuller Teen Center, 20
Bobby Goldsboro, 69
Bobby Keys, 108, 109
Bobby Parker, 21, 22
Boomer Norman, 46, 73
Buddy Holly, 16, 69
Buddy Miles, 69
Burnett Street, 44

C

Cactus Cafe, 88, 119
Calvin Russell, 78, 83, 91, 94
Cambridge Avenue, 15
Carol Simmons, 117
Casper Rawls, 89
Cathedral High School, 20, 25
Champ Hood, 71, 78, 80, 81, 82, 87, 89, 92, 99, 117
Charles Harrelson, 32
Charlies Attic, 57, 107
Charlie Pride. A, 113
Chewahwah Chase Records, 78
Chicago House, 88
Chicano gangs, 29
cholo, 25, 65
Chula Vista California, 105
Church, 117
Clark, 74
Clifford Antone, everyone knew, 65
Cody Heubock, 57
Coldwell Elementary School, 15
Community Gospel Choir, 71
Concordia Lutheran, 51
Continental Club, 30, 60, 81, 89, 93, 110, 117
Copacabana, 24, 25, 28, 29, 57
Costa Rica, 40, 41
Country Music Hall of Fame, 69
Curley, 43, 56, 57, 63, 86

D

Dallas Cowboy, 69
Dam Cafe, 62, 63
Dan's Liquor Store, 44
Dave Keown, 30
David Heath, 92
David McGriffert, 97
Debbie Norrad, 40, 45, 46, 47, 50, 52
Deep Eddy Cabaret, 60
Deep Ellum, 60
Deep South Productions, 78, 82
Del Castillo, 82
Derek OBrien, 30
Diamond Simon, 89, 106, 107, 115, 119
Dianne Fry Cortez, 103
Dick Clark, 36
Dime Box Texas, 73
Disco, 30, 34, 40, 46, 78, 120
Doak Short, 81, 82, 93
Don Walser, 66, 69
Double Trouble, 114
Downbeats, 22, 23, 24, 25, 26, 27, 28, 29, 34, 35, 37, 46, 48, 65, 66, 69, 70, 73
Downbeats, they were labeled as, 71
Dr. Neubert, 49, 50
Dyer Street, 16

E

Eddie Painter, 82, 89, 91, 106
Eddie Wilson, 111, 112
Eeyores, 70
Eeyores Childrens Show, 73
El Continental, 35
El Fronterizo, 35
El Kabong, 68
El Paso County Coliseum, 36, 37
El Paso County Jail, 31, 34
El Paso High School, 19, 26, 28
El Paso High School with only, 32
El Paso High School. H, 22
El Paso Independent School District, 32

El Paso Times, 30, 31, 35, 119
Elgin, 46, 52, 96
ELK Audio, 64
Emerson, 117
Emily Kaitz, 88
Emmajoes, 82
England, 40, 106
England. While living in HyWycomb Bullfiddler, 40
Eustolia, 82, 91
Eve Kuniansky, 64
Everly Brothers, 15

F

Fender, 22, 23, 45, 47, 52, 60, 66, 68, 106, 115
Fernando Castillo, 82
First Unitarian Universalist Church, 117
Flametrick Subs, 94
Floyd Domino, 78
Fort Bliss, 25
Fox Television, 71
Framus guitar, 21
Frank Zappa, 63
Frankie Avalon, 26
Franklin Avenue, 74
Franklin Avenue., 73
Franklin Avenue a short distance from Wallar Creek, 66
Freddie Fender, 115
Freddie Mendoza, 70

G

Garfield, 96
Gem/Lone Star Studios, 30
Gene Vincent, 15
Geoff Outlaw, 78, 82, 89
George Coyne, 78
George Jones, 118
Georgina, 65
Germany, 63
Gibson, 22, 115

Giddy-Ups, 119
Glynda Cox, 89
Grace Slick, 37
Greatful Dead, 89
Gretch, 54, 71
Guadalupe Street, 59, 64, 87

H

Hank Sinatra, 81, 87
Hank Thompson and the Brazos Valley Boys, 113
Hank Williams, 15, 39
Harley Davidson, 33, 62
Harley Superglide, 62
Harlingen, Texas, 81
Hells Angles from California, 30
Hep-C, 114
Herman Nelson, 121
Herman the German, 106
Hill's, 119
Hofner bass, 43
Houston, 43
Houston who was referred to Bullfiddler by Dr. Neubert., 49
Hunter Thompson., 114
Huntsville, 93
Hyde Park Methodist Church, 66
Hyde Park Tour of Homes, 46, 48, 70, 72

I

Ian Moore, 94
Illustrated Man, 63

J

Jack Knox, 65, 66
James Brown, 36, 37, 107, 119
James Merideth, 54, 55, 60, 61, 71
James, 60
Jeff Haley, 70
Jefferson Airplane, 37
Jefferson Starship, 37

Jerry Jeff Walker, 92
Jerry King, 120
Jessie Taylor, 86, 95
Jim Barry, 118
Jim Parish, 47
Jimmy Carl Black, 63
Jimmy Day, 69
Jimmy LaFave, 89
Jimmy R. Harrell, 60
Joe Ely, 78, 86, 87, 91, 108
Joe Hernandez, 65
Joe Phillips, 106
Joe Valentine, 45
John Casner, 83
John Conquest, 87, 88
John X Reed, 60, 92
Johnny Cash, 36, 39, 90, 92, 118
Johnny Nicholas, 30
Johnny Rivers, 56
Johnston High School, 49
Jon Dee Graham, 93
Joseph Vincelli, 69
Juarez, 16, 24, 27, 29, 30, 33, 34, 35, 37, 53, 88, 122
Juarez bars, 25
Jubal Clark, 82, 83
Jud Newcomb, 89
Judge Wilfred Aguilar, 110
Judge Wood, 32

K

Kahil Gibran, 105
Karaoke, 51
Kay student bass, 50
Kaz Kazanoff, 30
Keith Richards, 86
KELP radio, 36
Kerrville Folk Festival, 101, 102, 103, 122
Kevin Taylor, 30
King Carrasco, 51
Kinky Friedman, 123
Kristofferson, 93

L

La Palapa, 69
LaGrange, 46
lametrick Subs, 94
Larry Monroe, 83
Las Cruces, 16, 63
Leander, 66
Lee Chagra, 31, 32
Leslie Ann Warren, 96
Leti de la Vega, 74
Liberty Lunch, 93
Little Joe y La Familia, 65
Little Wheel, 52, 53, 119
Live Music Capitol of the World, 125
Llano, 81
Lobby Bar, 30
Local Flavor, 87, 88
London, 40
London Central High School, 40
Lone Star beer, 57
Long John Hunter, 30, 37
Los Destroyers, 25
Los Downbeats, 46, 48, 65, 66, 69, 71, 73
Los Indios, 81
Loyd Maines, 51
Loyd Maines and, 86
LSAT without really studying for the exam and was, 43
LSD, 26
Lubbock, 43, 44, 86, 87, 92
Lubbock-born, 86
Lukenbach, 84
Lupe Maldanado, 68

M

Manchaca, Texas, 66, 119
Manor, Texas, 47, 119
Mansfield dam, 62
Marbridge Ranch, 66, 72, 73
Marcella Elmer Garcia, 62
Marcella Garcia, 65

Marcia Ball, 69, 81, 92
Marcie Lane, 64
marijuana, 29, 31, 85, 93
Marty Robbins, 37
Marvin Dykhaus, 81, 82, 92, 99
Mary street, 74
Maryjane Ford, 118, 121
Merle Haggard, 97
Mesa Street, 29, 32
Mescalaro Indian Reservation, 34
Michael Ochs, 62, 64
Mick Jagger, 52, 108
Mike Och, 57, 66, 88
Moby Grape, 93
Mombo, 81, 82, 92, 93
Momos, 107
Mrs. Shapiro, 23
Mt. Christo Rey, 37
Muscle, 76
Muscle Shoals All-Star Horn Section, 76
Music City Texas fanzine, 69
Music from the Heart, 102
Musicians Union, 60
Musicians Performance Trust Fund, 71
Musicians Performance Trust Fund. I, 60

N

New Buffalo, 41
New Rose Label, 78
Nofziger, 88
North Yemen, 39, 40, 116
Nuevo Leon Restaurant, 108

O

Oklahoma City, 43
Old Fiddlers Waltz, 81
Old Ross, 119
Outhouse, 46, 50, 52, 54, 57, 63, 64, 70, 76, 82, 83, 89, 106

P

Palacios, 94

Papa John Creech, 37
Parrot Tracks, 78, 81, 82
Patos Tacos, 68
Peter, Paul and Mary, 122
Peter Paul and Mary, 19
Piano Tuning for Tone Deaf Dummies, 54
Ponty Bone, 78, 81, 86, 91, 92
Paul McCartney, 107
Paul Sessums, 78, 86
Peace Corps, 38, 39, 40, 117
Pete Seeger, 19, 122
Peace on Earth; Christmas Songs, 72
Poodies, 57, 71, 119
Poodle Dog, 115
Poor Yorick, 92
Precision bass, 66
Pure Country, 40, 45, 46, 47, 50
Pure Texas Band, 69

Q

Quakers, 118, 121, 122
Quero Rivera, 35

R

Rachel Rain, 82
Raindogs, 50, 70, 74
Rancho Vallejo, 81
Randy Fuller, 29
Ravens Garage, 50
Ray Benson, 41, 48, 69
Ray Price, 69, 97
Regan Marie Brown, 119
Richard Lasini, 20
Richard Patureau, 52, 54, 119
Rick Lane, 69, 104, 106
Ricky Nelson, 22
Rick Perry, 123
Robert Asocar, 78
Robert Casteneda, 69
Robert Ortiz, 115
Robert Quarter Moon Ortiz, 108
Robert Sarcinella, 62

Rock and Roll Emporium, 101
Rod Kennedy, 101
Rolling Stone from Texas, 69
Rolling Stones, 26, 35, 52, 108
Ron Erwin, 91
Ron Wood, 108
Ronnie Saltzmn, 18
Rosanne Arnold, 69
Rosas Cantina, 37
Rosedale Elementary School, 65
Roughcuts, 89, 107, 108, 115, 119
Roy Orbison, 16, 40, 56
Rudy Sanchez, 68
Ruidoso, 34
Ruidoso, 26

S

Safety in Numbers, 87
Salvation Day Parade, 71
Samandl, 49
San Antonio, 32, 43, 52, 70, 108
San Marcos, 51
Sanaa, 39
Saxon Pub, 93
Scholtz Beer Garden, 62
Second Ward, 25
Seton Medical Center, 92
Shelly King, 71
Shivas Headband, 78
Shorthorn Lounge, 45, 52, 56
Simon, 106
Smithville, 46
Sol Power, 81
South by So What, 94
South by Southwest Music Festival, 94
Southside, 112
Spellmans, 82
Spencer Perskin, 78, 91, 93
St. Edwards, 51, 54, 62, 65
St. Thomas Island, 34
Stanley Smith, 73
Stars Inn, 62

Stella F-hole, 18
Steve Crosno, 16, 36
Steve Fromholz, 101
Steve McQueen, 57
Stevie Ray Vaughn, 68, 86, 123
Stubbefield, 43, 86
Stubbs, 57
Sun Art Gallery, 89
Supernatural Family Band, 45, 52, 86, 91
Symphony, 49

T

T. Hale, 82
Tary Owens, 30
Temple Mount Saini, 15
Teri Hendrix, 51
Texana Dames, 92
Texana Dames and many others, 92
Texas Attorney General, 105
Texas Highway Department, 62
Texas Womans University, 93
Teye, 78, 79, 91
Theresa Locke, 60
The Bayou Bandits, 52, 119
The Dirgibles, 118, 121
the Dirgibles, 118
The Downbeats, 20, 22, 23, 24, 25, 26, 27, 28, 29, 35, 36, 38
The Frijolie, 37
The Go Cats, 106
The Grandmothers touring extensively all over Europe, 63
The Green Mesquite, 62, 87, 105, 107
The Jazz Pharaohs, 50, 70
The Kingston Trio, 19, 122
The Oaks, 71, 119
The Prophet, 105
The Resentments, 93
The Rib Ticklin Affair, 68
The Stallion Restaurant, 44, 52
The University of Texas, 51, 80
Thoreau, 117

Threadgills, 42, 52, 69, 71, 87, 89, 99, 106, 111, 112
Thundercloud Subs, 62, 104, 106
Timbuck3, 91
Tish Hinojosa, 70, 81
Tom Paxton, 101
Tom Shaka, 63, 64
Toni Price, 81, 89
Tony and The Tigers, 54, 55, 59, 60, 61
Tony and the Tigers, playing, 86
Tony Brassatt, 49, 50, 74, 88
Tony Masaratti, 54
Tony Masarotti, 70
Tony Price, 81
Tony Pulgese who had the, 54
Too Slim, 66
Towns Van Zandt, 54, 74
Traci Lamar, 92
Ty Grimes, 22, 25
Tye-Dye John Williamson, 91

U

Unitarian Church, 117, 118, 119, 121, 122
Unitarians, 121, 122
United States Army, 58
Urban Roots, 71
UTEP, 33, 34, 37

V

Ventures, 16, 28, 56, 63, 103, 105, 125
Victoria, 46, 52
Victory Bar, 30, 56, 107, 108
Victory Bar and Grill, 30, 56, 107, 108
Vietnam, 29, 35, 53

W

Waller Creek, 78
Walter Hyatt, 99
Wayne, 69
Wayne The Train, 69
WC Clark and other, 108
Weavers, 122
Whataburger, 114
Whitey Ray Huitt, 77, 82, 83
Wiccans, 121
Wildflower, 118
Willie Nelson, 54, 69, 74, 84, 96, 98
Willie the Fiddler, 62
Wilson Pickett, 119
Wolfman Jack, 16
Woodie Guthrie, 19

Z

Zerehade, 88